More Praise for Am

But I Love Him

"Ann and Connor inhabit every shade of hope, despair, confusion, ecstasy, longing, rage, and guilt with heart-breaking realism... powerful and compulsively readable."
—*Kirkus Reviews*

"Beautifully written and wholly believable... and marks [Grace] as a voice to watch in YA fiction."
—*Booklist*

"Intense. Scary. Heartbreaking. *But I Love Him* is a hard story to read, but one that needs to be told."
—*The Story Siren*

"*But I Love Him* is haunting, heartbreaking, and full of wondrous hope."
—*Sacramento Book Review*

In Too Deep

"Teens will empathize with [Sam], even as she digs herself deeper into the lie. An ill-fated romance and tense pacing add to the appeal."
—*Booklist*

"*In Too Deep* is an easy, engrossing, uncomplicated but not oversimplified read that will be enjoyed by male and female readers."
—*VOYA*

The Truth About You & Me

"Readers will get lost in Madelyn's brooding narrative."
—Foreword

No One Needs to Know

AMANDA GRACE

No One Needs to Know

flux ®

Woodbury, Minnesota

First Edition
First Printing, 2014

Book design by Bob Gaul
Cover design by Ellen Lawson
Cover image: 72664320/©fstop images/Vetta Collection/Getty Images Inc.

Flux, an imprint of Llewellyn Worldwide Ltd.

Library of Congress Cataloging-in-Publication Data
Grace, Amanda.
  No one needs to know/Amanda Grace.—First edition.
    pages cm
  Summary: Told from separate viewpoints, two seniors at an elite girls school grow close as they work together on a project and Zoey, a scholarship student, begins dating wealthy, troubled Olivia's twin brother, Liam, but romance blossoms between the girls, threatening both of their relationships with Liam.
  ISBN 978-0-7387-3625-9
  [1. Twins—Fiction. 2. Brothers and sisters—Fiction. 3. Sexual orientation—Fiction. 4. Dating (Social customs)—Fiction. 5. Social classes—Fiction.] I. Title.
  PZ7.G75127No 2014
  [Fic]—dc23
                                                            2014014111

Flux
Llewellyn Worldwide Ltd.
2143 Wooddale Drive
Woodbury, MN 55125-2989
www.fluxnow.com

Printed in the United States of America

Acknowledgments

Firstly, this book wouldn't exist if it weren't for my editor, Brian Farrey-Latz, who suggested I write outside my normal box. Thank you for believing I could pull it off, and for pushing me when the first draft didn't quite work.

Secondly, thank you to Sandy Sullivan, who always manages to catch the trouble spots. I appreciate your keen eye!

Thirdly, thank you to my kind, amazing agent, Bob Diforio, who must operate on 2.5 hours of sleep. I don't know how you do it.

And finally, thank you to B and D, who never complain when I disappear into my office for a few hours to write. At the risk of sounding like Kelly Clarkson—life would suck without you. Love you both.

OLIVIA

Before I even open my eyes, I know something's off. My bed's too stiff, my pillow is too thick...and I can hear my twin brother, Liam, snoring.

I want to roll over and cover my head with my blanket, but judging by the light trying to pry its way through my eyelids, it's morning. And a school day. Ugh. I still haven't quite adjusted to September.

I groan and sit up, glaring in the direction of the sound. My brother's sitting on the other sofa, an arm slung over his eyes, his mouth open as he snores. The TV screen is overtaken by a screensaver; random portraits of wild animals glide across the screen, one after another.

We'd been chain-watching *The Walking Dead* on Netflix when I zonked out.

I reach over to the coffee table, scoop up a handful of popcorn, and hurl it at Liam. Only one kernel lands in his mouth, but it's enough. He snorts and coughs and then abruptly sits up, spitting the popcorn onto the ground. His sandy-blond hair is sticking up at odd angles, making me giggle.

"Thanks, dude," he says, glaring at me through slitted eyes.

"*De nada, señor*," I say, swinging my feet to the floor and then heading to the kitchen for a glass of water. While it fills from the dispenser, I study the flier stuck to the fridge. "I get to choose our Friday night movie."

"I know, I know."

I don't miss that it's more of a grumble than an agreement.

"You can't complain if it has subtitles," I add, tracing the name of one of the movies with my finger. It's French.

My glass full, I walk to the windows and peer out at Puget Sound. In the distance, a ferry steams toward our shoreline, carrying people from Vashon Island. We've lived in the penthouse at Point Ruston for two years and I'm still getting used to it. I mean, the elevator, the parking garage, the Brazilian-cherry floors, sure. The view? It's just as awe-inspiring every time I peer out the windows. Our old place, a beautifully restored Victorian mansion, was farther up the hill. The water view wasn't quite as *in your face*.

"Pretty much everything at the Grand Cinema has subtitles," Liam mutters, finally getting off the couch and walking up next to me, still rubbing at his eyes.

I ignore his whining. "We should go kayaking on Saturday. It's supposed to be hot."

"I'm busy," he replies. "Maybe next weekend."

I want to ask him what he's busy with *this time*, but I resist.

"Maybe by next weekend the weather will suck." My eyes roam the skyline, taking in the high, fluffy clouds. It's been hot all week. Well, hot for Washington State anyway—mid 80s, blue skies, the feeling of the days stretching on and on. "Summer's pretty much over."

"So?"

I frown. "So, if we miss the good weather, it'll be months before we get out again. Come on, please? You never want to hang out anymore."

Liam rolls his eyes, then looks down his nose at me like I'm being childish. "We're going to the movies tonight, aren't we?"

"Yeah. Okay." I hate the needy tone of my voice, but I can't help it. There's just something... *off* about our friendship lately, but he won't acknowledge it.

"You nail down the quarterback position yet?" I ask, walking back toward the kitchen.

"Coach will pick on Monday." His reply is surprisingly half-hearted.

I study his face. "You still want it, right?"

"Yeah. Of course."

I chew on my lip. I'm not buying it, but my brother is obviously not in the mood to talk. "Okay, well, good luck." I set my cup on the counter. "Meet me at the theater at six?"

"Sure," he says. "See ya then."

I leave him in the kitchen, walking to my room for a quick shower before heading off to another mind-numbing day of school.

————

"Marriage of convenience," my best friend Ava announces as she arrives at our lunch table. She sets down a Diet Coke and drops onto the creaky bench.

"Uh, you mean like an arranged marriage?" I ask, popping a baby carrot in my mouth.

"Exactly." She dumps her food out of a brown paper sack, and I just barely manage to catch an apple that rolls across the table. I toss it her way and she catches it without a blink. "Wouldn't that be nice, if some level-headed person could just pair you with the right guy and you didn't have to put up with all this dating garbage?"

I laugh. "Yeah, because I'm never going to find a boyfriend in an all-girls school. I'd take an arranged *date* at this point."

Ava grins. "Right?"

"Why is arranged marriage on your mind? Is Ayden being a jerk again?" I ask.

"No. It was last night's article," she says, yanking open a bag of potato chips. "It was about how arranged marriages aren't just in India or whatever, but that a lot of industrialized countries still have them."

"Ohhhh." Every day, Ava's dad makes her read one longform article from a major magazine or newspaper—we're talking *Time*, not *Seventeen*—and then discuss it at the dinner table.

I reach for another carrot. "I don't know. If it was up to your dad, you could end up married to a total creep who looks really great in pictures. You know, for the campaign trail or whatever."

"But at least the creep would attend the charity brunch my mom is coordinating this Saturday, unlike Ayden, who's trying to ditch it." Ava sits up straighter, fingering the strand of pearls on her neck. "I mean, they're not *that* bad. I got to meet the president last year."

"Yeah, no, they're really that bad," I say.

"Whatever." Ava grins because she knows I'm right.

"Do you want to work on our reading list this weekend? I'm completely overwhelmed and we're, like, only two weeks into the semester. I'm so screwed."

Her nose scrunches up. "Ugh, *no*. CliffsNotes. They invented them for a reason."

"There's still the essay assignment, and the million calc problems, and the chemistry lab—"

"Whoa, take a deep breath and quit worrying about it, will you? You sound like you're about to break out in hives," she says.

I sigh. "It wouldn't kill you to work with me on homework. I mean, one of these days Mrs. Emery is going to realize you've never read *any* of the assigned reading, and this is your third year with her."

Ava smiles, wide and triumphant. "I look forward to that

day. Then I can remind her that my dad pretty much paid for the library that houses said books, and she'll have to shut up."

I toss a carrot at her. "You're terrible."

"Terribly awesome," she says, flinging the carrot off her green plaid skirt—which is standard issue for all girls at Annie Wright School. "You're just jealous I'm so cool and collected. Unflappable...unflustered...composed..."

"Oh come on, Ava," I say. "You've gotta worry about school at some point."

"Please. If I'm going into politics like my dad, I can't get worked up over freaking homework."

I prop an elbow on our lunch table and rest my chin in my hand. "Have you done *any* of it?"

"Yeah, of course. I'm totally done with the mock campaign posters for leadership."

I snort. "Naturally."

"I'm so gonna ace that class. I've been waiting *years* for it."

I pop another carrot in my mouth, wondering how many I can eat before I turn orange, and let Ava's words go in one ear and out the other. She can blather forever when it comes to leadership class, and before I know it, the bell rings. She disappears almost immediately, waving goodbye to me over her shoulder.

My stomach growls as I stand, shoving most of my lunch back into my bag. It's not that I'm trying to lose a ton of weight, but a pound or two would help my gymnastics performance. It's a small price to pay, really.

I try not to look at the stack of homework in my backpack, or the three textbooks I need to bring home, but it's impossible to ignore the tightness in my chest as I remember how behind I am already. I don't remember school being this overwhelming this fast before.

I zip my backpack shut, wishing I could push away the stress as easily as I can bury books in my bag, and then head across the cafeteria, striding straight toward the restroom.

Halfway there, a small group of sophomores blocks the path, completely oblivious. I pause, waiting for them to see me, but they're too busy talking. I only have a few minutes to duck into the bathroom and get what I need from my bag, out of the view of the student body.

"Excuse me," I announce, annoyance lacing my tone. "Maybe you could take your little conversation out of the pathway?"

The girl nearest me, a redhead, grabs her backpack. "Oh, uh, sorry." She moves just far enough that I can squeeze past them and make my way to the door of the restroom.

I'm relieved to find it empty. I set my backpack on the countertop, then fish out a little purple pill box.

Just as I'm about to open it, a girl from my history class, Zoey, waltzes through the door, her torn-up sneakers squeaking on the tile floor. The shoes look ridiculous with the schoolgirl outfit, like some lame attempt to make our standard uniform look punk rock.

I freeze, standing there like a deer in headlights, my fist clenched around the pillbox.

Zoey pauses, her gaze flicking to my hand and then to my face and back again. I must look like I got caught with my hand in the cookie jar.

After a few heartbeats of nothing but staring back at her, I let out a jagged breath of air.

One side of her mouth curls up in a mocking smile as she glances down at my fist again. "Diet pills, maybe? I mean, you don't really *seem* like the type to go for the harder stuff…"

My face flushes and I shove my hand back into the pocket of my backpack, dropping the box inside. I zip it shut, panic tightening in my chest. "I don't do drugs, you idiot. I'm a gymnast. I can't poison my body like that."

They're prescription, so it's not like they're *drugs* drugs. Not the kind of thing girls like Zoey probably do.

"Hmmm…" She tips her head to the side, tapping one black-lacquered finger on her chin in an annoyingly exaggerated gesture. "And yet I've caught you red-handed doing *something*…" She brightens and claps her hands together. "Oooh, pregnancy test?"

I let out a snort of ugly laughter. "I'm a freaking virgin. I don't even have a boyfriend. And I swear to god if you start spreading rumors…"

She screws her crimson-painted lips up to the side and ignores my words. "But then a pregnancy test is too big to fit in your fist like that, so—"

"Just shut up, okay?" I grab a paper towel and dry off my hands. It's just my luck that our school's resident pariah was the one to find me in here. She'd probably love to hand the title off to me and dust her hands of the whispers that follow *her* around like smoke trails a fire.

Then Zoey turns around, reaching for the bathroom door. I scramble over to her and grab the strap of her messenger bag, yanking her toward me just as her fingertips brush the door handle.

"Whoa," she says, stumbling back and turning to face me.

"Just forget about it," I snap.

Her expression morphs from triumph to something else. Sympathy? Ugh. The last thing I want is Zoey Thomasson's *sympathy*.

"Huh," she says. "So the girl who has everything has something to hide."

I do nothing but stare into her eyes, willing her to forget it. She saw nothing. She knows nothing. But I can't get my heart to stop spasming painfully against my ribs.

"All right, all right," she says, breathing it out on a reluctant sigh. "Your secret's safe with me, princess." And then she pats my cheek, smiles, and pushes past me, disappearing into a bathroom stall.

I don't trust her—*no one* trusts her—and I stand there for a long moment, uncertainty swirling in my stomach. I don't think she actually saw what was in my hand, so there's nothing for her to tell. But I screwed it all up with that panicked, frozen reaction. Now she knows I'm hiding something, and that's enough to freak me out. I leave the bathroom without another word, simply because I'm not sure what else to say.

The late bell rings before I'm halfway to Chem, but I can't bring myself to care.

ZOEY

Olivia Reynolds has a secret.

Those five words have been rolling around in my head for the last hour and a half, and part of me regrets that I didn't just knock her out and dig into that ugly Coach backpack of hers to find out what it is. One decent punch to the nose and I bet she would've keeled right over.

It was that wild, cornered-animal look that stopped me. The building panic gleaming in her eyes.

The girl who beams from every yearbook photo, who has single-handedly filled one of the trophy cases in the hallway, has a whole lot more going on in her head than I'd ever expected. And it's almost... *almost* enough to make me like her. You know, if she weren't such a self-entitled bitch.

I push my way through the crowd, heading toward the only class I share with Olivia—history. I make it through the door with only seconds to spare and sink into my chair, glad I'm several rows behind Olivia. She currently has her back to me and is chatting with Ava, her BFF, the one I would like to strangle with my bare hands.

Mr. Nelson walks to the front of the room, a stack of paper in his hand. "All right guys, settle down. I'm returning your quizzes today. Some of you have some ground to make up, but I've got good news for you: we're getting into our first big project of the new semester. It represents twenty percent of your grade for this term, so you're going to want to spend some serious time on it. Especially those of you who didn't fare so well on our first quiz."

He's walking around the room now, setting quizzes face-down on desks as he goes by. When he reaches my desk, my breath hitches in my throat. I *need* a solid grade in this class, in *every* class, or I lose my scholarship.

This place—Annie Wright School—is the only good school I've ever gone to. Inside these walls, I forget about the hellhole I call home. But if I get even *one* C, I'm out. And even though I'm pretty damn smart, even though I work hard, the pressure constantly makes me second guess.

I hold my breath, flip the quiz over, and instantly grin. A-. I can handle an A-.

"Okay then," Mr. Nelson continues. "The project will be done in pairs. You'll be choosing one time period in American history. You'll then report on a historic event from two different perspectives. Choose two people involved and showcase their viewpoints. Be creative. For example, you could show the Civil War through the eyes of the president and a slave, or show a battle from both sides. You can write a compare-and-contrast essay or two fictional letters or create a skit, anything along those lines. Basically, I want to see how two people with wildly dissimilar perspectives view the same event."

He turns to the board and starts writing *DIVERSE PERSPECTIVES ON AMERICAN HISTORY*, and the class starts to hum. Someone's chair screeches as they slide over. Four rows up, Olivia and Ava smile at each other.

Ah, yes, the familiar sting of rejection. I haven't had an automatic-partner in three years, ever since . . . well, in three years. I don't want to think about why every girl in this school refuses to acknowledge me.

"Settle down, folks. I will be *assigning* partners."

I sigh. With a bit of luck, I would have ended up as the odd one out and I could've done the project alone. Twice the work, sure, but none of the drama. Last spring, in junior English, I got paired with Charlotte Vincent, Ava's cousin. She refused to get together outside of class and I did the entire project myself. I just showed up and handed her cue cards for her speaking parts.

"I've got eleven pairs of numbers in this hat, so choose a number and then find your match," Mr. Nelson says, walking up to the first row. As he works his way back to me, I glance around, trying to decide the best case scenario. There's a new transfer student who wasn't at Annie Wright when everything went to shit. She's probably heard about me, but she might not care about my apparent super-power of stealing boyfriends.

Mr. Nelson finally gets back to my corner, and I'm the

last to choose a number. Around me, the desks are already screeching across the floor as the students find one another. And as I unfold my scrap of paper and find the number three on it, the transfer student is already chatting with her new buddy.

I stand up and look around, grabbing my ratty messenger bag and heading toward the front, to where a few people are still comparing numbers. But the closer I get, the more the dread spins through me.

Because Ava just walked off with her partner, and the only one still alone is Olivia. Great. She'll probably do the same thing as Charlotte and ignore me, and I have no time to do both sides of the project. I'm barely staying afloat.

When she looks up and meets my eyes, her face flushes and she stiffens.

"Number three?" I ask, holding it up. She doesn't speak, just flashes me the matching number on her slip of paper. So I drop into the seat next to her, spin the desk to face her, and meet her eyes.

She stares back, and a thousand things seem to fly between us. She's questioning me, challenging me, judging me. And suddenly I want to defend myself.

"I meant what I said in the bathroom earlier," I find myself saying. "I mean, I won't—"

"*Shut it*," she says, cutting me off. She darts a nervous glance over at Ava. Wow—girl is dodgy. "Look, you and I aren't friends, and this project isn't going to change that. We'll settle on a topic and do a simple essay. I'll write my paper immediately. Then you can look it over so that the compare and contrast aspect is clear, and you write yours. I'll review it to be sure my paper still stands, and we're done."

I stare back at her, wondering how much of this has to do with whatever she's hiding and how much has to do with hating me, with believing everything she's heard about me. Behind her, Ava is darting glances our way, as if to be sure Olivia is being rude enough to me.

"No talking necessary then, huh?" I say, anger igniting. "You've got it all figured out, as always."

"What's that supposed to mean?"

"You're a planner. A color-coder." I wave my hand over her binder. "You know. A control freak."

"Look. Unlike you," she snarls, her eyes sweeping over me as if she can tell by my appearance I'm some wastoid loser, "I care about my grades, and I'm not going to let you screw this up. So let's just settle on a topic and get to work, okay? We don't have to like each other."

Of course she thinks I don't care about my grades. Of course she thinks she's better than me. Olivia has no idea what it's like being one bad grade away from losing my slot in this school. Her parents have no problem ponying up the cash to send her to this place, with its brick façade and manicured lawns and ridiculous tuition.

"Clearly," I mutter, wondering why I ever once wanted to be her friend. I actually used to admire her. It seems like a lifetime ago.

I flip open the textbook. We skim over a few chapters in silence, the only sounds coming from the turning of the pages. The tension settles around us like a fog, but I can't think of anything to dispel it. I'm the enemy. Because her friend hates me. Because I caught her doing... something in the bathroom.

I should just tell her I don't even know what the hell she was doing in there, but part of me likes that she's so on edge. It makes her almost tolerable.

"How about the abolition of slavery?" she says, glancing up from her textbook. The look in her eyes has morphed back into the cool, composed Olivia I've come to know and loathe.

"Too obvious," I say.

"The Boston Tea Party," she says.

"Too boring," I say.

"The signing of the Declaration of Independence." She's flipping rapidly through the pages now, scanning the chapter titles.

"Overdone."

She tosses her hands up in the air, and I kind of like that her frustration is already bubbling over. Pushing her buttons is proving way too easy. "What do you suggest, then?"

"Everyone's going to cover the major events, but they're overlooking the simpler things. I say we compare and contrast the socioeconomic standing of two Americans during a rapidly changing time in history. A factory worker or a farmer or something, and someone wealthy. Make it less about an event and more about everyday living."

She stares at me, and it almost looks like awe. Like she thought I'd go, *Erm, I dunno, how about, like, whatever?* Does she really take me for such an idiot that saying anything intelligent has rendered her speechless?

"When?"

"The Industrial Revolution," I say. "The changes would've had a big impact on daily lives, both in a factory and at home. Think of the ways the workplace must have changed. Imagine the new inventions rich people could buy. There's a lot to work with. The compare and contrast practically writes itself."

Olivia's finally warming up to the idea, nodding her head and flipping to the corresponding section in our text. "Who writes about which viewpoint?"

I fight the urge to roll my eyes. "You can relate to receiving new inventions the second they're available, right?" I ask, glancing down at the iPhone sitting at the edge of her desk. "So you take the yuppie and I'll cover a factory worker."

Olivia makes a disgusted noise in the back of her throat. "Just because my family's wealthy doesn't mean I don't know what it's like to be a hard worker."

"Right. Next time you want to cover my double shift in place of your little tumbling events, just let me know."

She narrows her eyes and opens her mouth, as if to argue, but I cut her off.

"I think we covered that we're not going to be friends, so what do you care what I think of you?"

She crosses her arms and leans back in her chair, like she's just remembered that we hate each other. "I don't."

"Exactly. You're more into ruling with an iron fist."

"What's that supposed to mean?"

I scoff. "You know, stomp on people? Rule through fear? Instead of earning respect, you demand it."

She snorts. "Oh please. You're the one being judgmental and rude."

"I'm serious. When you walk out of this classroom, take a look around. Look at the people who will avert their eyes just because you look their way. Walk right up to someone less popular, less perfect, and see if they smile at you or shrink away."

"Oh come on. People aren't *afraid* of me."

"Right."

She stares right at me, her jaw line tight, and I know I've annoyed her, pushed her just far enough that she's going to bite back. "Fine. Know what? I'll do it. But you have to too."

"No one's afraid of me," I say, rolling my eyes at the mere suggestion. "I'm a joke to them."

"That's exactly my point. You're totally paranoid because you're stuck in the past. Newsflash, nobody cares anymore, but you still skulk around this school like a kicked dog."

I swallow. She doesn't know the extent of what Ava put me through.

She leans back, smiling at my obvious unease. "Talk to a few people. I bet you could be normal if you weren't so paranoid that people are making fun of you behind your back."

"Fine. You know what? You're on." I yank my desk away from her and pull out a blank sheet of paper, quickly scrawling down a bullet-point list of ideas and topics to cover for my side of our essay.

And for the rest of the class, Olivia doesn't say a word.

———

An hour later, before my last class of the day, I pull myself up onto the window ledge and slide my crappy old phone out of the front pocket of my backpack. I can't remember whether I'm supposed to work today, but I've got it programmed into my calendar.

Just as I unlock the screen, Olivia rounds the corner, all smiles. With the way she curled her hair today, it's really bouncing around her shoulders. She's alone, her thumbs hooked into her backpack straps as she meanders down the hall like she's got all the time in the world. I bet she could show up late to any class and get out of a tardy.

As her eyes leisurely rove the faces of our classmates, it hits me.

My jaw drops. She's actually doing what I dared her to do. Olivia freaking Reynolds, who hardly even spoke to me until today, is actually rising to my challenge.

Holy shit.

My mouth goes dry as I watch her pause, scanning the hall. There are two girls from the school band in the corner, gripping instrument cases as they lean up against their lockers, lost in conversation.

I grin as Olivia sets her eyes on them and then clicks into motion, heading their way. I'm dumbfounded—not just that she's doing what I told her to do, but that she has no idea what's about to happen. My only regret is that I'm way too far away to hear, because this is bound to be some damn good entertainment.

She walks up, and one girl's eyes widen. Her face pales as she glances over at her friend.

When the friend turns to see Olivia Reynolds standing directly in front of her, she sort of jumps, and the back of her head knocks into the locker.

I don't have to be an expert lip reader to make out *Oh, uh, hi,* coming out in a desperate jumble of words.

I grin and drop my feet down, then jump off the window ledge and inch closer to the action as Olivia tips her head to the side. She must be speaking, but her back is to me and the crowded hallway drowns out her voice. The two girls nod, their expressions serious, and then Olivia turns around just as the two girls share nervous glances.

Olivia takes two steps and then stops short, staring across the hall at me.

I grin, pop a hand on my hip, and mouth *I told you so.*

Something flares to life in her eyes, but I don't know what it is. Surprise, anger...confusion? I blow her a teasing kiss and then turn and walk away, feeling stupidly triumphant.

Olivia just got one rude wake-up call. I can hardly believe she even attempted that, but those two girls, their reaction...so flawless.

I'm around the corner, still grinning to myself, when I remember her own challenge to me. Her preposterous assertion that people don't even care about my reputation as a boyfriend-stealing slutbag. I'd dismissed the whole conversation about three and a half seconds after we'd finished it. But now I've seen Olivia living up to her side of the bargain. And maybe I have to return the favor and actually talk to someone.

Or not, and just say I did. I don't have to tell her who I supposedly talked to.

I push my way through the crowded halls, my eyes trained on the floor, as always, and make my way to my final class, Spanish. No one should be made to conjugate verbs at this time of day, when we're all brain dead after five other classes, but some part of me actually likes Spanish. It takes every ounce of willpower to follow our instructor, who insists on speaking *only* Spanish inside the classroom, despite the fact that this is only a second-year class and sometimes none of it makes any sense. Then she's forced to write out the instructions in English on the board, like somehow that doesn't count since she didn't speak the words aloud.

We have assigned seating, alphabetically by our Spanish names. I picked Rosa on the first day, for no other reason than that the name reminded me of Rosa Parks, and she was a pretty badass chick.

I slide into my chair and pull out the homework we were assigned yesterday, glancing over the worksheet. It had been an easy task, really, writing the Spanish words next to a variety of modes of transportation.

Samantha, a girl I used to do projects with during freshman year, drops into her seat beside me.

I swallow. "Hey, Sofia," I say, using her Spanish name.

She blinks and meets my eyes, like she just realized I was sitting here. We've been sitting beside one another for two weeks. Have I not even said hello to her yet?

"Uh," I say, suddenly realizing I have nothing intelligent to say. "What did you get for number ten? It was totally hard, right?"

She glances down at her homework, and then opens her

mouth to say something, when her friend "Camila" sits down in the row in front of us.

"Zorra," Camila quips. Sofia tries not to laugh, but it comes out like a strangled cough.

Slut.

Camila just called me a fucking slut. In Spanish.

My cheeks burn and I try to come up with something to say—some way to burn her back—but I come up empty. So I jerk my gaze away, staring down my homework.

Slut.

I am never going to live it down. No matter what Olivia has to say about it.

I was right about her, and I'm right about *me*.

OLIVIA

He forgot.

I can't believe he forgot.

I'm sitting on the curb in front of the Grand Cinema, trying to ignore the clouds that have rolled in and the raindrop that just fell on my cheek. Rope lights outline movie posters behind me, but it's not dark enough yet to cast shadows.

He forgot.

I don't know why it burns like this, like some deep, lingering betrayal, but as I glance at my phone again and confirm that the movie started ten minutes ago, I can't escape the way my chest hurts.

We haven't missed a Friday night independent movie in ... two years?

I text him for a third time: *Where are you?*

I count to thirty before tucking the phone back into my

purse. Liam is completely MIA. I pull the two tickets out of my pocket and rip them, again and again and again, growing even more upset as I shred them so many times, they're pretty much dust when I'm done. I hold my hands out to the breeze and let the paper flutter to the cement at my feet.

That's my day, right there, ripped to shreds and forgotten in the gutter. Between stupid Zoey Thomasson and those two girls in the hall and my brother's failure to show, this is officially the worst day ever.

There's no way Zoey's right. I know she thinks she was, based on that little show in the hall, but they could've just been surprised, not afraid. If they were *actually* afraid of me, they would've, like, run or something. It's not as if I can even be intimidating. I'm five foot four. And no one clad in a schoolgirl uniform is scary looking. It's physically impossible.

I stand up and step onto the sidewalk. I walked up here after gymnastics practice. It's like a mile and a half, but it was such a pretty afternoon, the late-summer sun waning, and I thought the fresh air would help me unwind.

But I'd planned on having a ride home, since our condo it a full three miles away. I could call a cab, but I'm so angry . . . so wound up . . . that I don't want to bother.

Instead I dig into my purse, pulling out the purple pill box that Zoey almost saw. I fish out one pill, pop it in my mouth, and swallow without needing a sip from the water bottle buried somewhere in my enormous handbag.

I know it's not instantaneous. Xanax doesn't work like that. But just knowing it's in my stomach, that it'll kick in fifteen minutes or so from now, is enough to let me rake in a long breath and feel my shoulders unwind.

I stomp away from the theater and head toward Stadium Way, wondering if my brother somehow lost track of time and is still at school. But that's ridiculous. Classes at Stadium High end about the same time as they do at Annie Wright.

For the millionth time, I wish Annie Wright were coed at the high school level. It's coed up to junior high, but after that, boys aren't allowed. Since there aren't any good private schools for boys around here, Liam goes to public school, but my mom insisted I finish out my education at Annie Wright.

So this is our fourth year apart, and every year, I swear, it's like Liam and I grow a little more in opposite directions.

He used to be more like me, kinda preppy or whatever, but now he's hanging out with all these skater kids and going to the skate park, and he downloads all this weird music I've never even heard of. If you saw us standing next to one another, you'd never think we were related, with the way he dresses.

I don't know if it's because I don't fit in with his new group of friends, but I'm not automatically invited to stuff anymore. He has this *entire life* outside me now, and it freaks me out.

I pass his school, with its enormous turrets and gothic lines, all made famous in the movie *10 Things I Hate About You*. It looks more like a castle than a public high school.

It's quiet. If my brother decided to hang around after class with his buddies, he's gone now.

So I get to walk home.

Alone.

ZOEY

I'm in the kitchen, my arms covered in bubbles as I scrub the last dirty pan, when the door flies open and Carolyn bursts in. I twist around to yell at her—there's already a hole in the drywall from the door knob—but when I see her, I freeze.

Tears are streaming down her face, her nose is bright red and snotty, and she's got a black eye.

Someone gave my ten-year-old sister a fucking black eye.

I rush over, water and soap creating a trail behind me, and reach out to touch her cheek. She flinches away, but I follow her and wrap her up in a hug. "Oh Carolyn, what happened?"

"T-t-t-t," she stutters, choking through the tears.

"Take a deep breath," I say, rubbing her back.

She obliges, raking in big lungfuls of air as her trembling shoulders calm. I wait in silence, my arms still wrapped around her, until she's ready to talk, and then I lean back and rest on my heels.

"Talia hit me," she says.

Talia. Of course it was Talia. The girl has been bullying my sister since the first day of class, when Carolyn showed up in her favorite *Littlest Pet Shop* T-shirt, which apparently is *so* not cool at ten years old. Every day, there's another story of Talia hurling insults at Carolyn.

And no one seems to give a shit.

"At school? Why didn't a teacher call me or Mom right away? Or help?"

"It was after. When I was waiting for the bus."

"She just ran over and punched you?"

"She was bothering me all day," Carolyn says, her words coming out in hiccups of breath. "She kept calling me a baby, telling me I cry like one too. I told Mrs. Bryant, but she never does anything!"

My heart twists and my stomach clenches and I want to kick something or punch someone or scream at the lousy teachers at my sister's school.

If we didn't live in the Hilltop neighborhood—or if only Carolyn could get a scholarship to Annie Wright like I did—she wouldn't be stuck at such a crappy school. Or if we could just move about a half mile away, to where the assigned school is *anything* but Hilltop...

If only, if only, if only.

This is why I haven't committed to a college yet, haven't even started the applications. Because when it comes down to it, I'm probably going to end up getting some kind of full-time job after graduation, just so I can kick in a little more toward rent and get us the hell out of here before something even worse happens to Carolyn.

I can't leave her like this.

I won't.

"At least it's Friday," I say, wiping away her tears. "You don't have to deal with her for a couple of days. We'll figure something out, okay? I promise."

"I don't want to go back," my sister says, the desperation in her voice mirroring the emotions swirling in my stomach. "Don't make me go back."

The lump in my throat grows a mile wide, but I muster the ability to smile in a way I hope is reassuring.

"Come on," I say, standing. "Let's go watch cartoons. I'll let you spoil dinner with some popcorn."

She sniffles again, then wipes her eyes and follows me the three feet it takes to get to the living room, where she flops down onto the couch. I go to our adjacent bedroom and dig through the stack of DVDs sitting on our battered dresser. I got them all for ten bucks at a garage sale, and we've seen all them, but it doesn't matter. Any cartoon featuring an animal is fine with Carolyn.

———————

Two and a half hours later, she's smiling, or at least as well as she can without wincing. The bag of frozen peas she's been using to ice her face has mostly melted, which I guess means it's halfway to being ready for dinner.

I've sat next to her on our ratty couch this whole time,

despite feeling like I could climb out of my own skin. When the door creaks open and my mom walks in, still wearing the blue polo shirt and apron that comprise her maid uniform, I jump off the couch and signal her to meet me in the kitchen. Since the lights are low and the TV is still on, my mom walks right past Carolyn without noticing her eye.

She drops her purse on the table, her eyes trained on mine like she knows I'm about to drop a bomb.

"Carolyn got hit again," I whisper.

Her face pales and she glances over her shoulder. "Is she okay?"

"Does a black eye count as okay?"

Mom's jaw drops and she freezes for a moment, then spins and starts toward the living room, but I grab the ties on her apron and yank her back.

"Don't freak out. She's calmed down now," I say, glancing over her head to be sure Carolyn's not watching. "But this isn't working."

"What's not working?"

"This!" I hiss. "We can't live here if it means sending her to Hilltop Elementary."

"I'm doing the best I can," my mom says, the weariness creeping into her voice. "If we could afford to move, we would have done it already."

"She barely survived last year. This year is worse. We *need* to move," I say. "If we can find a place on the other side of Division, she'll be able to go to—"

"We can't afford to rent over there. You know that."

"I've been saving a little money. I could help with the deposit."

"And then what?" Mom asks, sinking into a chair at the kitchen table. "It doesn't help to move in if we can't keep up with the rent."

"Can't you scrape together enough to get us to June? After I graduate, I'm going to work full time—"

"You'll end up like me," my mom says, her voice falling. "You can't just start working, Zo. That's not what we've always talked about. You need to focus on you, and college."

"How am I ever going to focus knowing Carolyn's still here?"

"It'll help her if you help yourself first."

"By the time I get a degree and can get a real job, she'll be sixteen and the damage will be done. That school is going to ruin her. I don't even like *walking* through these neighborhoods, and she spends all day here!"

"What do you want me to do? I've been applying for better jobs all over town. No one even calls me," Mom whispers, rubbing her eyes.

"You're going to have to do better," I say, reaching for my hoodie. "I gotta get out of here."

I shove my arms through the sleeves and then slip out the back door before my mom can protest. If I spend one more minute in that house, I'm going to go crazy.

I zip the front of my sweatshirt as I find the sidewalk and head down the hill, away from the crappy Hilltop neighborhood, the place we've lived for the last few years. I turn onto Tacoma Avenue, meandering past the courthouse and the strip of bail bond stores, past McDonalds, and then a few blocks later, I finally hit Division. This one road stands between Carolyn and a new elementary school, but who am I kidding? It's a road and a pipe dream away.

My mom's been working as a hotel maid for so long, I don't think she knows how to be anything else.

I don't have a destination, so I just keep walking—past the sprawling Wright Park, where Carolyn spent half her summer playing in the waterpark sprinklers, and then over to a Chevron gas station. Inside the brightly lit store, I fill a hot chocolate, pay for it at the register, and then I'm outside again.

There's a bench next to the ice freezer, so I sit down, sipping at the drink, trying to decide what I'm going to do next. I can't go home. I'll go nuts inside those four walls, which are more of a cage than anything else could possibly be.

Stars twinkle to life, but I'm the opposite. I feel like I'm dimming. Day by day, minute by minute, the pages in my book are being written, and they all point to the same ending: stupid, crappy job like my mom; crumbling, shitty house forevermore. Maybe if I'm lucky I'll marry some deadbeat like she did and send my own kid to a gang-riddled, underfunded school.

I don't know how to change it, though. I can graduate with honors from Annie Wright, maybe get a little bit of a scholarship for college, but my mom's wrong. Me leaving won't help Carolyn, not in time to make a difference. She's too sweet, too soft, to survive in that school much longer.

A deep rumbling makes me glance up. I see a dark blue pickup, something from the sixties or the seventies, pulling up to the pumps. It sparkles and gleams under the bright station lights. Two guys climb out of the cab, one of them dressed in a royal blue and gold letterman's jacket from Stadium High.

I pretend to be super interested in my hot chocolate, but as they approach the doors, I glance up. The boy in the letterman's jacket looks over at me, flashing an easy, megawatt smile as he enters the store.

I'm hot from the inside out. He has pretty, warm blue eyes and messy brown hair, and I can't help but wonder what it would feel like to run my hands through it.

I'm still sitting there, nursing my hot chocolate, when the bench creaks and he's sitting next to me, leaning back and stretching his legs out in front of us. My eyes linger on his DC sneakers and baggy jeans.

They're more skater boy than jock, totally at odds with his jacket.

"What's up?" he asks, like we're friends, like it's a normal thing to do.

"Um, nothing?"

"Why are you sitting at a gas station all by your lonesome?"

I smirk, glancing over at him with amusement. "Is that the sort of thing that works for you?"

He blinks. "What?"

"That line," I say, crossing my arms. "Do girls fall at your feet?"

Grinning, he says, "Generally, yes."

"Interesting."

"You're unimpressed," he says.

"Oh no, I'm incredibly impressed."

He laughs. "I meant it, though. What are you doing just sitting at a gas station?"

I lean back on the bench, my shoulder touching his, my legs stretched out like his are, except mine don't reach the edge of the walkway. "Nothing better to do."

"Well, we're headed to my house to play pool. You can join us."

Whoa. This guy is forward. "How do I know you don't have a dungeon or a torture room?"

He pretends to ponder my question. "I mean, we only own the penthouse. I guess there could be a dungeon somewhere in the building."

"Penthouse?"

"At Point Ruston? Down by the water?"

Pretty boy has money.

"I know it," I say. I saw a flier, once, blowing in the wind near Annie Wright. Those condos *start* at five or six hundred thousand dollars, for little one-bedrooms without a water view. The penthouse must be well into the millions. "But I don't know you."

"That's cool. Just thought I'd offer. You look..." His voice trails off and his eyes sweep over me. My face heats up as I wait for him to finish his sentence. "Bored."

Oh.

The door behind him swishes open, the same ding-ding that I've been listening to for the last several minutes. *Ding*

ding, another minute of my pathetic life burned up waiting for something to change, to give, but it never does.

"Ready," the other guy says, and then pauses when he sees me sitting next to his buddy.

"Last chance," he says, standing up. "Unless a gas station is more your thing for Friday nights. I mean, maybe it's a better option. I can't promise you Twinkies and disgusting hot dogs."

Against every logical fiber of my being, I find myself standing. Following him. Climbing in the truck.

It's only when we pull away that I realize I don't even know his name.

OLIVIA

I stoop down and pick up my discarded iPod, which was tossed aside in favor of some indie punk song that's blasting from the surround-sound, vibrating so hard it's rattling my eardrums. I grit my teeth as my brother's little skater buddy, Rusty, swings a pool cue around like it's a baton, circling the table and surveying the few balls left on the felt.

I didn't even know they were home until I walked out of my room and saw Rusty pouring himself a drink. Apparently my brother's in his room or something. Judging by his total lack of urgency to talk to me, he hasn't even realized he stood me up. Instead, he was hanging out with this slacker doing god knows what.

Rusty takes a shot, then lets out a big whoop when one of the balls streaks toward the pocket.

"I'm going to get something to drink," I announce, even though the idiot probably doesn't care. I spin on my heel, my shoes clacking as I exit the room. When I'd realized the house was under invasion, I'd promptly changed from my yoga pants and T-shirt to a cute argyle mini and heels, though god knows why. I don't want to impress Rusty. He probably has the IQ of a monkey.

I stalk to the kitchen, disappointment and anger and the ever-present tension boiling in my stomach as the music dies down behind me. I'm staring into the fridge, trying to decide between a Diet Coke and another Xanax, when something clatters behind me.

I straighten my sweater, brush my hair back over my shoulders, and turn around, prepared to take on my brother.

But it's not him.

"Surprise, surprise," Zoey says, grinning from ear to ear.

My stomach sinks. She is the *last* person I want to see right now.

"I guess I should have put two and two together," she says. "In my defense, 'Reynolds' is a common name. I had no idea you two were related. And, you know, personality wise, he's kinda your opposite. Less bitchy, and more—"

I clear my throat and she stops. "And I had no idea you knew my brother."

"I don't," she says.

"Then how do you know his last name is Reynolds?"

"His letterman's jacket," she says.

I turn back to the fridge, reaching for the soda. The ball's in my court, but I can't decide what to do next—how to handle the interloper in my kitchen.

So what if she was *almost* right with her stupid challenge.

She still doesn't know what was in my fist in the bathroom. Doesn't know I can barely survive without anti-anxiety pills.

She doesn't know me at all.

"Want a drink?" I hold out the soda.

"Got something hard to mix it with?"

"Whiskey," I say, pointing to a bottle on the counter, presumably something Rusty dug out of our parents' collection.

"Perfect." Zoey plops down on the stool at the other end of the granite island, reaching for the bottle and one of the glasses left out. After dumping the whiskey into the cup, she holds her hand out, awaiting the can.

I hand it to her, and it takes her only a moment to pour it into the glass and take her first sip. She closes her eyes for a moment, as if savoring it, before looking at me again.

"Soo … how long have you been Liam's sister?" And then she giggles, like the joke is hilarious, and I wonder if maybe she's had a few drinks before this one.

"Wow, you're sooooo funny. You should be a comedian."

"Nah. I'm sure you've got me figured out—I have no plans of rising above the working class. Really more of the factory worker type. It's a shame I didn't live in 1790, like my character. I think I could really master a loom." She takes another swig of her drink. "But I bet that doesn't compute with you. You're probably thinking, what—Harvard Law? NYU Medicine? First female president, guaranteed to inspire world peace?"

I stare at her for a long moment, completely unamused. I'm not smart enough for any Ivy League. My parents used to harp on me constantly, that I wasn't living up to my potential, that I needed to spend more time on homework if I had any hope of meeting their expectations.

I suppose that's one upside of their absence. They travel so much—mostly for work, sometimes for fun—that I don't have to hear their nagging. I guess they gave up on me and are pinning all their hopes on Liam, who achieves A's as naturally as he throws the football.

"*Why* are you in my kitchen again?"

"Waiting for your brother. He wanted to take a shower," she says, taking the last big gulp of her drink. When she sets the glass down, the ice rattling in the empty cup, her deep red lipstick glistens. Her cheeks already look pink, the alcohol setting in. "Apparently he was skateboarding. *After* football practice. Maybe he's into sports or something?"

"Oh." I narrow my eyes. That's why Liam blew me off? To go freaking skateboarding with his buddies? Isn't football enough for him? "And you're telling me he didn't use his famous line about showering together to conserve water?" I ask. "I guess he's not too interested in you."

She grins, not the reaction I'd expected. It's a real, genuine smile, and it transforms her features from hard and unapproachable to complete girl-next-door. It's almost like the moment the curtain is peeled back in *The Wizard of Oz* and you realize you were never really meant to see the Wizard at all, that seeing him ruins the carefully crafted image he created.

"He tried. I declined."

I blink. "Hmm … you might be smarter than the last three."

She laughs, not even partially offended by my insinuation that his girlfriends are a dime a dozen.

I shouldn't be so rude, but I can't believe he picked Zoey over me. I mean, he always does this—gets a girl and gets infatuated for a few weeks—but she's not really his type.

"So, if you're so smart, why are you after Liam?" I ask, waiting for the next round of entertainment. At least this conversation is better than watching Rusty play pool in the other room. "Because he's not going to commit, you know."

She shrugs. "It's not like I'm looking to be some guy's Happily Ever After. I'm cool with Happy For Now."

Funny. All I've ever want is Happy, period. Now, Ever After, In Between. *Something.*

"Do you go out with a lot of 'happy for now' sort of guys?" I ask.

"Back off," she says, irritation suddenly lacing her tone. "Weren't you trying to convince me earlier today that people didn't see me that way anymore?"

I purse my lips, swallowing, hating that she's right. The first chance I had, I threw her reputation in her face.

I raise my hands in a surrender pose. "Sorry."

"You're just like all the others, you know. So happy to laugh and make snide remarks."

I just stare.

"Oh, whatever, don't act wounded. With all of your amazing accomplishments, last year's yearbook probably had to be extended by a dozen pages. President of FBLA, captain of the gymnastics team, leader of the debate team..." Her voice trails off.

Everything she said is true, yet the way she's saying it—like I've done it all just to show off, that I didn't have to give up every free moment to achieve those things—aggravates me. "Ah, so you've got me pegged, huh?"

"Hey, just like I said, it's pretty obvious you like being on top of the totem pole, even if you have to climb over people to get there. And you realized I was right, didn't you?"

I grit my teeth and stare her down, willing her to, I don't know, spontaneously combust.

Instead, Zoey looks smug as she traces the rim of her glass with a finger. "I've seen you and your little friend at your precious little lunch table. You've cobbled together just the right things to broadcast the image of perfection. Take your preppy little skirt, for instance. It fits right in with the…décor." She waves her hand around the room. "You wear our required skirts all day every day, same as me, and yet you don't take the chance to relax when you're home."

I cross my arms. "I'm not a cardboard cutout."

"No one said you were. I'm sure there's some substance behind your pretty little façade. I'm just waiting to see it."

My jaw drops.

"Don't look so offended. I'm just calling it like it is. If you thought I was wrong, you'd be angry, not shocked." She shrugs, but her eyes still don't leave mine and I find it hard to look away. I no longer feel guilty for being such a bitch to her earlier.

"Like I said, Olivia. *Image*. You know all about it."

And with that she walks away, disappearing down the hall.

ZOEY

Image.

What the fuck was I even doing, blasting Olivia about image? Like I don't spend more time shredding my clothes than she does applying her pastel lipstick. At least she has her shit together, even if it all does seem a little fake.

Then again, I'm still not sure what happened in the school bathroom, so maybe she doesn't actually have her shit together. My money is still on diet pills. No one gets that skinny without cutting corners.

I knew her place would be just like that—all pompous and shiny, overstuffed but simultaneously hollow. The kind of home that screams money, oozes it at every turn.

At least it turned out to be a fun evening. Snobby little Olivia disappeared somewhere after our conversation and the boys decided to play beer pong, and Liam kept teasing me but not in an asshole sort of way. In a flirty way, which was almost as intoxicating as the beer. For one shining evening, I wasn't such a loser.

And once he'd ditched his letterman's jacket in favor of a T-shirt with a big *Ghostbusters* logo, he almost seemed like my type. Like he wouldn't mind hanging out somewhere low key instead of a place like their penthouse.

No wonder I didn't guess that Olivia was his sister. They're polar opposites.

And now, as I walk home, my head spins in a way that makes it hard to think about pretty much anything.

Perfect.

It's only a few miles to my house, but those few miles might as well be a few hundred for all the changes I encounter. The new construction on the waterfront gives way to the Victorian mansions in old town, which transition to neat and tidy homes with their perfect little shutters and postage-stamp-sized lawns, and then those turn into darkened apartment complexes with rusting chain-link fences and dogs barking.

It's here where I can't help but slump my shoulders, hunching into my sweatshirt and pulling the hood up over my hair. When I make it to our tiny box-shaped house, I cross the weed-infested lawn and climb the cement steps, stopping to pull out my key and unlock the door.

My mom is lying on the couch, her eyes closed as the TV flickers in the darkness, some kind of late night infomercial. I've never understood it, but she can stay up all night watching infomercials even though she can't afford to order anything. I guess it's the closest she gets to shopping.

I pick up the blanket that's slid off her body and tuck it around her shoulders and feet. She stirs but doesn't wake.

It's like my buzz wears of instantly as I look at her, so tired she didn't even make it to bed. I shouldn't have yelled at her earlier and stormed off. She really is doing her best, and she's all me and Carolyn have.

I pick up the plate and cup on the coffee table and take it to the kitchen, setting it down as quietly as possible.

Then I head to the room I share with my sister.

I creep through the door, resisting the urge to sweep her hair out of her face and see how dark her bruise has become. Instead, I climb into bed and pull the threadbare blanket up to my chin.

I wonder if Olivia realizes how good she's got it. If anyone could grant me just one wish, it would be that Carolyn was her sister and not mine.

She deserves to live like Olivia does.

OLIVIA

"Must be nice," I say, studying my brother as he walks into the living room, an energy drink in hand.

"What?"

"Being a guy." I step into his path and gesture at his clothing and hair. "Rolling out of bed and throwing on some old T-shirt, and still looking decent."

The words aren't all that biting, but my tone is. I'm still pissed at him for blowing me off.

He gives me a gentle nudge and I kind of bounce off the wall as he walks past me. "Whatever. You're the one who decides to slather all that crap on."

"Oh, come on, you know it's a double standard." I follow him as he pushes the French doors open and steps out onto our balcony. The warm sea breeze welcomes us.

"Somehow I doubt it was some dude who created makeup,"

he says, leaning forward and resting his forearms on the railing. "So don't blame me."

"Says the guy whose girl-of-the-moment resembles a raccoon."

He flicks a glance over at me. "It wasn't that bad, was it? I thought she was kind of cute."

"Obviously, since you decided to pick her up like a stray cat and bring her home."

"I like her. Might keep her around for a bit."

"Famous last words." I sit down on an Adirondack chair, adjusting the back so I can recline.

"What's that supposed to mean?"

"I give her a couple weeks," I say, grabbing the *Cosmo* magazine I discarded on the side table a couple of days ago. It's still a little chilly to be outside, but it'll warm up. "Sorry, but you're not exactly the relationship type, and that girl is one hot mess. Too much for you to deal with."

Liam downs the rest of his drink in one big gulp. "Eh, whatever. I guess we'll see."

I grin at the annoyance in his voice.

"You know, you could at least have texted me last night."

"Why?"

"Seriously?" My anger spikes again. "You blew me off. I looked like a complete tool sitting there waiting for you."

"Sitting where?" he asks.

"The Grand Cinema!"

His jaw drops and I watch the range of emotions cross his face. "Ohhhh."

"Yeah. Oh."

"I'm sorry," he says. "I completely spaced."

"Whatever."

"No, really, I'm sorry. I didn't do it on purpose."

"I know. I'm sure you found some super-amazing staircase or handrail and couldn't leave until you aced it."

His silence is all the confirmation I need.

"I'll let you make it up to me," I say, leaning back again and squeezing my eyes shut. "Let's skip class on Friday and head out to the cabin. Then we'll be there all day Saturday, for our birthday, and we can come home on Sunday. A whole three days at the cabin. If this weather holds up, we'll be able to swim. I mean, Ava can't make it, but you can invite your friends just like always."

He doesn't speak, so I crack one eye open. But he's still standing at the railing, his back to me, his hands loosely clasped as he leans on his forearms.

"Liam?"

"I was thinking of going to the casino for my birthday. You know, turn eighteen, break in the ID..."

My chest constricts. "But we always go to the cabin," I say, and it sounds like an accusation, that same neediness creeping in. God, what is with me?

"I know. But this is different. We're about to be adults."

I don't know why it feels like my heart has climbed into my throat. This shouldn't be that big of a deal. It's just... our parents began taking us to the cabin when we were kids, and then once they started leaving us to our own devices, we just carried on the tradition ourselves. Ten years now, we've celebrated our birthday the same way.

46

And now he's clearly already decided. Given it a lot of thought. Made plans.

"What casino?" Emerald Queen Casino is in Tacoma, a ten minute drive from our place. Even though spending my birthday there isn't what I want, I could do it. Show up for a few hours, play some blackjack or bingo or something.

"Quinault. I was thinking of getting a room on the water."

Oh. That's way better than stupid old Emerald Queen. I could walk the beach, enjoy the sand...

"That sounds fun," I say, reluctantly, giving up the idea of our tradition. After all, we're getting older. We don't have to do the same thing forever. "I guess we could do that."

That's when he finally turns around, and the look of pity on his face is like a dagger to my heart. "I'm going with the guys, Liv."

My eye sting, almost instantly. "Why can't I go?"

"Why can't you just make your own plans? I've shared my birthday with you all this time, and now I want to hang out with my friends. It's not a big deal."

"Our birthday is in a week," I point out. "You could have told me before now! Ava's going to L.A. with her mom. What am I supposed to do?"

"I don't know! You're an adult too. I'm sure you can figure it out."

And then he leaves me there on the balcony with only the sun for company. I try to be mad, but I can't muster the anger when all I feel is hurt.

I've spent my whole life with my brother as my best friend.

I don't know who I am without him.

ZOEY

Burgerville is the bane of my existence. More specifically, the hideous blue visor is the bane of my existence. No matter how many times I adjust it, it seems to just loosen up, and then it slides forward and falls into my eyes.

"I hate this stupid thing," I mutter, shoving it back onto my forehead.

"You and me both, kid," says my coworker Rita as she walks past. "I'll be in the walk-in for a little bit taking inventory. Think you'll be okay?"

I survey the mostly empty dining room. "Yeah, I can handle it."

I finish wiping the countertop with a bleach-laced rag and the bell near the door beeps. I glance up from my work, but the visor falls down again, obscuring my view of whoever just walked in the door.

Screw it. "Welcome to Burgerville, how may I service

you?" I say, in a fake cheery voice, like serving up burgers made of forty-seven ingredients is the pinnacle of my existence.

Someone on the other side of my visor snickers, so I shove the thing back onto my forehead.

Oh. "Uh, hey," I say, when I meet Liam's gaze.

Next to him, Olivia crosses her arms and shoots an annoyed look at her brother. "Ah. Now I understand the sudden, earth-shattering need for a greasy burger. Get me a Diet Coke," she says, striding away.

"Hey, I'm just a method writer," I call after her. "This gig is part of my research into the lives of factory workers."

She pauses for a second and narrows her eyes, like she almost believes me, but I can't keep a straight face. She ends up just shaking her head and walking off.

When I look back at Liam, he gives me a lazy half-smile. "Hey, so—"

"How'd you know I worked here?" I ask.

He cocks one bushy eyebrow, and for a second I wonder if that's how Olivia would look if she didn't wax and tweeze every last stray hair. "You told me."

"Oh." God, I'd been really drunk. I was so hung over when I woke up yesterday that it nearly carried into today.

Burgerville is just far enough up the hill that most kids at Annie Wright or Stadium High never wander in. And if they do, it's always via the drive-thru, which I avoid like the plague. Guys like Liam don't bother coming in and sitting down at a place like this.

"So, uh, what can I get for you, other than the Diet

Coke?" I punch the soda key on the register and wonder if there's a subtle way I can ditch this dumbass visor without looking like I'm doing it for him.

"Give me the double-burger combo, too."

"Onion rings or French fries?" I ask, hating my life. I feel like a walking, talking cliché, a poor kid working a dead-end job and asking, "Would you like fries with that?" But this job is a means to an end.

I'm just not sure where the end is.

"Onion Rings."

"Okay. With Olivia's drink, it's $6.42."

He hands me a hundred, and a few moments later I'm handing him more cash than I see in weeks.

Liam shoves the change into his pocket haphazardly, like he's used to carrying wads of bills around, like it's not a big deal if a twenty ends up on the floor.

"I'll bring out your food when it's ready."

"Great," he says, plastering on an easy smile. And in that instant I know that's what life is to him—easy. He waltzes through it without a care in the world, throwing footballs and riding skateboards, every day just like the last. I don't know what he plans for his future—if he's a perfect little brainiac like his sister seems to be—but I know it doesn't matter. Whatever he wants, it's his.

I wonder what it's like to live that way, to have this never-ending burden lifted.

I watch him a second longer as he strolls away, his letterman's jacket hugging his shoulders, *REYNOLDS* blazed in gold at the top, and then I turn back to my job. I salt the fries and dump a new basket of them into the grease, the oil hissing.

"Classmates?" Rita asks, setting her inventory sheet on the counter next to my register.

Rita's thirty-four years old and has worked here for nine years. I have a hard time looking directly at her, because I know every time I do, I'm going to see myself staring back. She's me as an adult, if I don't figure out how I can make something of myself without leaving Carolyn behind.

A few minutes later, I'm plunking Liam's burger on the tray and walking toward the siblings, balancing Olivia's Diet Coke on the edge. I don't breathe until I've managed to set it down without spilling it all over her silk polka-dotted blouse.

"Do you have a break coming up?" Liam asks, reaching for an onion ring. I don't have time to tell him it's fresh from the fryer before he bites in and winces, fanning his mouth.

The edges of Olivia's lips curl but she doesn't say anything, just sips at that Diet Coke of hers.

"Um, yeah. I guess."

"Cool. Sit down with us," he says.

"Uh, just a second," I say, and then hustle back to the counter. "I'm going on break," I call to Rita, then slip off my mustard-stained apron and toss my visor onto a hook near the counter.

Moments later, I'm sliding into the chair next to Liam, wearing just my red polo shirt and black pants. Liam reaches over, and I freeze as he slides his fingers over my hair. "Your bangs are a little jacked up from that hat," he says.

"Uh, thanks."

"You still look cute, though," he adds, like he realizes he's just insulted my craptastically good looks. Olivia's lips thin into a line, like she's trying not to laugh at him. Or me.

Yeah, probably me.

"Uh, thanks," I say, and then inwardly cringe that I'm just repeating the same stupid things over and over. Screw this. I'm not going to let him intimidate me. A week ago I didn't even know he existed. "So, what've you been up to?"

"Eh, yesterday I went skateboarding again," he says.

"Oh? How'd it go?"

"Ew, don't ask him that," Olivia interrupts. "I can't handle another dramatic retelling of his rail slide."

"Hey, it was pretty epic."

"Right," Olivia says. "I'm sure the X Games will be calling any minute."

"Fine, don't believe me."

I watch their verbal sparring, pretending not to be bothered by it.

And I'm not bothered. I'm jealous. I wonder what it would be like to be able to joke around with Carolyn, to not have all of our shit hanging over us. Instead I'm stuck icing her eye and watching garage sale cartoons.

"Olivia just wishes she could skateboard like I do," Liam says, turning to me. "What about you?"

"Skateboarding? No."

"Any sports?"

No. Sports cost money. "Uh, no. Not really a sports person, I guess."

"See, Liv? You're not the only human being in a five mile radius completely incapable of mastering a sport."

"Gymnastics is a sport," she says. "Quit acting like it's not."

"Sports involve balls or wheels."

"Yeah, and we've established I have ovaries."

I snort and her eyes slice over me, taking in my clothes, my unruly hair, my utter lack of makeup. I sit up taller and stare back, waiting for it. Anticipating the biting remark. She meets my gaze and we stare into each other's eyes for a heartbeat longer than is comfortable.

"I don't know why you're laughing at me. Unless you've got balls."

"Liv!"

She blinks innocently at Liam. "What? I don't see why you're so into her. You don't normally scrape the bottom of the barrel." She stands, her chair screeching across the tile floor I get to mop later. "I'll wait in the car. The smell of cheap food is leeching into my clothes."

Then she spins around, her perfect hair whipping around her shoulders, and strides out.

"Yikes. Sorry. She's not usually like that. She's just pissed at me and she's taking it out on you."

"Why's she mad at you?"

He sighs. "I accidently stood her up on Friday night. And then yesterday I told her I'm kind of ditching our usual birthday plans."

"Our? So you're not just brother and sister, you're twins?"

"Yeah. And we've always celebrated it together."

"So why not this year?"

He pops an onion ring in his mouth, and I get the distinct impression he's trying to buy himself time. "The thing is, I love my sister, but lately I kind of feel like the asshole mother bird who has to shove its kids out of the nest because they're not attempting to fly."

"That was very poetic of you," I say as I reach over and steal an onion ring.

"I just thought she'd grow up and expand her horizons, but instead she's kind of getting more and more clingy."

Olivia Reynolds, clingy? That doesn't fit my picture of her. She's too confident, too self-assured.

He chomps another onion ring. "So, do you want to hang out tonight?"

I blink. "Tonight?" Thank god I didn't react with what I'd wanted to say, which was—*me*? So maybe he did come here just for me. Not for his undying need for a greasy burger. I kind of expected Friday to be a one-time deal, though. Surely he *has* better prospects than me. It's not like *his* school is gender-segregated.

"Yeah, tonight."

"I work until ten," I say.

I expect him to frown or react, like *oh poor you, working late on a school night,* but he just nods. "Oh. Sometime this week? Tuesday or something?"

"Uh, sure. I guess so."

"Great," he says, wiping his fingers on a napkin. "Where can I pick you up?"

A white-hot streak of embarrassment shoots through me. "I'd rather just meet you there. Uh, wherever *there* is."

"Dorky's," he replies.

My jaw drops. "You like Dorky's?"

Dorky's Barcade is the closest thing to paradise for me and Carolyn. I set aside twenty dollars from every paycheck and take her there on Sunday afternoons, if I don't have to work. We order a basket of grilled cheeses for five bucks and use the other fifteen on quarters. If I'm careful, we can spend two hours there, forgetting about our troubles. Watching my sister light up, laugh, enjoy herself in that place is what gets me through each week.

But I hadn't really pegged Dorky's as Liam's style. They're into old school stuff like Super Mario Brothers and Pac-Man and Teenage Mutant Ninja Turtles, and they play '80s movies. But now that I'm getting to know him, seeing past the football and the penthouse, maybe a place like that is totally up his alley.

"What's not to like?"

"I mean, I love it. But I thought maybe you had..." My voice trails off.

His mouth quirks up on one side. "What, like my own arcade?"

I crinkle my nose. "Sorry. No, I mean, better places to go."

"No one is too good for Dorky's."

I grin. "I agree. Meet you there at six?" That'll give me enough time to feed Carolyn dinner before I hand her off to my mom and walk down to the arcade.

"Sounds like a plan to me," he says.

"Zoey, a little help?" a voice calls out. Rita. I glance up and realize there's a line up at the counter. I've been so wrapped up in our conversation I hadn't even noticed it.

"On my way," I say, standing. "See you Tuesday?"

Liam picks up his burger. "Yep. See ya then," he says, casual-like.

And as I walk away, I can't help wishing it was Tuesday already.

OLIVIA

My floor routine is getting worse.

I don't know how that's possible, since I'm practicing non-stop, but it's true. I just feel clumsier and more out of whack with every pass. Grace, fluidity, power... it's all dwindling.

Two years ago, I was the best girl on the team.

Last year, I was *one of* the best. I was there to help make up the points when we were a little short.

But this year is different. The freshman are amazing, and I haven't quite gotten back onto the same shape I was last season. I should have worked harder over the summer, instead of taking that trip to Europe with Liam and our parents. I gained four pounds and didn't work out. God, I shouldn't have relaxed like that.

I chew my bottom lip as I wait for Arianna to finish the cartwheel/back handspring/back tuck that ends her floor routine. She's brand new to our team and already nipping at my heels. In this sport, age and experience isn't a positive.

Swimmer Michael Phelps was in his twenties when he got all those Olympic medals. Meanwhile, the fantastic seven—the USA's first gymnasts to win a team gold? Between fifteen and eighteen.

Not that I'm Olympic quality or anything. That ship sailed. A long time ago, much to the bitter disappointment of my mom.

I'm always disappointing her. And Dad.

And me.

There's no way the football players over at Stadium High feel this kind of pressure. They seem to get better every year, rising through the ranks until they're seniors, when they're captains and quarterbacks and whatever else.

I've also sacrificed more every year. Every month. Every day. Just to be the best, and all I'm doing is freaking failing.

There's one hazy memory I think of at times like this. I'm in the sunny breakfast nook at home, before we sold the old Victorian. My mom's in the kitchen, bacon sizzling in a pan. I can't see my dad, but I can hear the hum of an engine, and every few minutes he whizzes by on the riding mower. And every time he appears, he's making a different funny face. Sticking out his tongue. Pulling down his eyes. Making a fish mouth.

Liam and I are across from one another at the little bistro table, and I've got a whole bottle of chocolate syrup, and I'm squeezing as hard as I can, hoping I end up with a more-chocolate-than-milk concoction.

I know the memory has taken on an unrealistic golden glow, the kind of memory one thinks of as "the good old days" without acknowledging that the old days sucked just as much as the new ones. I know my mom and dad probably started—or ended—the day fighting about one thing or another. I know Liam and I probably spent the whole afternoon with Anna, the au pair who spent more time with us than our parents.

But I know that in that one moment, I wasn't thinking those things. I was laughing at my dad, so hard that I missed the milk entirely and dribbled chocolate syrup on the table. I know that I ate the bacon my mom cooked without calculating how many slices I could have without topping my 200 calorie limit for breakfast.

It's this stupid, desperate longing—this rose-colored-glasses way of looking backward—that makes it hard to concentrate on gymnastics, yet somehow makes everything I want seem more possible, too. Like maybe if I was happy once, I can get there again.

I blink away the memory and swallow an intense desire for bacon as I look back at Arianna. When she steps out of the way, I square my shoulders and move to the corner of the floor, ready to begin.

I'm already warmed up, but as I wait for Coach Vicks to finish talking to Arianna, as I wait for my music, I twist a few times, then hop a few times, trying to limber up.

I haven't nailed this routine yet. The final tumbling pass throws me every time. And if I don't figure it out soon, Coach Vicks will insist on me going with something simpler.

And if I simplify my routine, that means I can't get the maximum points, and one of the freaking freshman will probably beat my scores. They'll be the indisputable best.

And I'm not okay with that.

Coach finally turns away from Arianna and the girl bounds past me, her dark pony bouncing.

"You're never going to finish that last rotation," I call out to her. "You don't have enough speed on your takeoff."

She glances over at me, her face falling before she jogs away toward the uneven bars.

Jesus, what the hell is wrong with me? I close my eyes and take a deep, calming breath, pushing away all of Zoey's accusations. I'm not a bitch. I was trying to be helpful.

I open my eyes, my stomach twisting. I nod at Coach Vicks, and she signals for a girl nearby to hit play.

The music starts as a low hum, but rises soon thereafter and the beat kicks in. I smile, that same blinding, toothy, fake smile I always use, as I raise my arms and flash them back and forth. Ever since I saw *Bring it On* I've wanted to refer to them as jazz hands, but that's silly.

A moment later, I rock back and then accelerate forward in a burst of speed, flying across the floor. A cartwheel turns into a handspring turns into a back tuck, and I'm spinning in the air.

I land easily. It's a combination I've done since the third grade. But it still makes my adrenaline spike, still gives me that surge of triumph.

I'm on top of the world.

I cartwheel into splits and throw in a bit of showmanship,

smiling and rocking to the beat. I roll backward, then I'm on my feet again. My hands flutter back and forth with the rhythm of the music and I pick it up with my hips, too, periodically pointing my toes. In competition, I need these moments to catch my breath and recenter myself before the big tumbling run.

I make my way back to the corner, then turn, rake in a deep breath, and take off again.

Cartwheel, handspring, back tuck, twist...

And I miss.

Down I go, slamming into the ground with so much force that I don't stop there. My body tumbles one more turn, until I land face down.

And even though the wind has been knocked from my lungs, all I can think of is...

I failed.

Damn it.

I failed.

"Olivia!"

The voice is enough to make me squeeze my eyes shut. It's the tone, really. The disappointment, laced with a tinge of anger.

A tone I've heard all my life.

I rake in another desperate breath as the burn in my lungs ebbs, and then I pull my knees under my body and stand up. Like I didn't just slam into the floor at a million miles an hour.

"Yeah?"

"What's *with* you?"

"I know," I say, groaning under my breath. "I was short."

"You were beyond short."

I bite my tongue and nod. "I'm sorry. I just didn't sleep well last night—"

"No excuses. You were off all last week, too. You want your spot on this team, you gotta earn it."

My chest is still heaving as I try to catch my breath. Gymnastics has been a part of me since I was five. She can't boot me. "I know, Coach."

"Do you want it?"

I grit my teeth to keep from snapping at her. Jesus, of course I want it. I wouldn't put myself through all this otherwise. "Yes," I answer automatically.

"Then show me," she grinds out. "Again."

"Yes, Coach."

And so I return to the corner.

And I start over. My smile is even more plastic this time, and I want to just skip to the end. I want to try that final tumbling run again and again and again, until I get it right and this burning anger and frustration in my gut goes away.

This time, as I reach the pivotal moment, I rake in the deepest breath I can and stare across the floor with a laser-guided focus. And then I explode. From my hips, my feet...I fly into the cartwheel.

And in that very first touch of my fingers to the floor, I know.

I know I'm about to nail it.

My body twists, turns, spins...and as the final rotation ends, as my legs extend, I'm not surprised to find the floor kissing my toes.

I'm not surprised to find my balance centered as my arms fling upward, as I finish with a grin. A real one this time. I just nailed the hardest routine of my life.

For the first time in a long time, triumph races through my veins, and I'm happy.

ZOEY

I feel stupid as shit as I wait for Liam outside Dorky's, picking the flaking purple paint off my nails. It's Carolyn's polish, some crappy two dollar bottle I bought her for her birthday a year ago. I had no idea how much it sucked until now.

Not like I painted my nails just for Liam. That would be stupid. I was just bored, really.

Luckily, the nail polish turned out to be a two-step boredom cure: ten minutes of painting, thirty minutes peeling it off.

We agreed to six o'clock, and it's six twenty now and I'm starting to look like an idiot. I'm so pissed that I let myself believe he'd be here. *Stupid.* No one is ever there when they're supposed to be. And I don't normally give them the chance to disappoint me.

Stupid stupid stupid.

I push off the brick wall I've been leaning on and yank

the strap of my messenger bag over my head. Liam Reynolds let me down. SHOCKER. The guy seems to get everything he wants, and I bet he has a lot of options. He probably ditched me in favor of some perfect girl from Stadium High with huge knockers and way less baggage.

I would literally kick myself if I could. For a second, back at Burgerville, I believed he was interested, and that was a dumb thing to do.

I stride down the sidewalk, not looking up until I'm at the corner. And when I do look up, there's someone walking toward me, halfway through the crosswalk.

Liam.

Not gone, not forgotten. *Here.*

"Sorry," he begins. And he actually looks sheepish, his full lips getting all puppy-dog frowny. "I was running late, and maybe I was a little excited to see you. So I may have been speeding. And gotten pulled over."

"Bullshit," I say, my guard still up. "That's got to be one of the oldest excuses in the book."

He digs into the pocket of his jeans and pulls out an amber-colored slip of paper that he thrusts at me. "Seriously. Those cops down on Ruston Way are not into apologies."

I narrow my eyes, then yank the slip out of his fingertips. I unravel the paper, scanning over it.

Fifty in a thirty-five. One hundred ninety-two dollars, courtesy of Officer Glassman.

He's not lying.

And I hate the warmth I feel in my gut as I hand the

paper back to him, smiling for the first time in hours. "I don't think I'm worth two hundred bucks."

"I think you are," he counters, shoving the ticket back into his pocket. Briefly, I wonder what it must be like to shrug off a two-hundred-dollar expense. "And it's my mission to make you believe it."

"Riiiiiight," I say, smiling flirtatiously. This…whatever we have…it's okay, as long as I don't get too invested. Let the rich boy take me out on a few dates, wine and dine me or however that saying goes.

"But I guess that'll have to wait, seeing as I've made us late for a game of Donkey Kong."

"A pity," I say, not shrugging his arm off as he settles it around my shoulders. It's warm and protective and feels stupidly nice. I forgot what it was to be wanted.

He steers me back in the direction of Dorky's and soon we're inside, assaulted by the sounds of dozens and dozens of video games.

"Want anything to eat?"

"I'm okay," I say. "I had dinner with my sister."

"I didn't know you had one."

He stops next to the change machine, feeding in a twenty dollar bill. The cup overflows with quarters, which he scoops up and hands to me, filling my palms.

"Yeah. Carolyn," I say, shifting my hands so I don't drop any of the coins. "She's ten."

He feeds in a ten dollar bill, then scoops up another handful of quarters and drops them into his own pockets. "Is she at Annie Wright with you?"

"No, Hilltop," I say, before I realize it.

Shit.

He cringes. "Seriously?"

"Yeah. We, uh, live up there."

"Why didn't you invite her here with us?"

I study his face, my fingers still curled around the quarters, trying to figure out if this is some kind of pity offer. If he's suddenly realized I'm legit poor and feels sorry for us. I can handle a friend, but I don't need some guy rescuing me.

"Um, she was busy," I lie. Carolyn would have loved to join us. Maybe I can save half these quarters for her, bring her down tomorrow.

"Oh. Okay. Uh, let's go play. I bet we can beat the Simpsons game."

I follow him, trying to shove all the quarters into my pockets without dropping any, wondering how it is that someone like Liam ended up in my life.

Because good things never happen to me.

And Liam is a good thing.

OLIVIA

When I open the door to our condo on Thursday, the first thing I hear is a *crack* sound.

Our pool table.

Great. I'd kind of hoped Liam's friends weren't going to be over today. I wanted to try and beg my way into going to Quinault with him, but I can't possibly grovel in front of the other guys.

But... I also can't spend my birthday alone. That's pathetic. I'm *this close* to asking Ava to let me go to L.A. with her, even though she's going there to support her mom's charity-of-the-moment.

When I round the corner, I find Liam stooped over the table just like I expected, but he's not playing the guys.

"Zoey," I say, before my brain kicks into gear.

"Shhh," Liam says. "I'm about to beat her in pool."

I find my mouth curling up into a smile. "Ah, she wasn't dumb enough to bet you, was she?"

Her immediate scowl tells me otherwise.

"Aw, shucks, are you hustling your own girlfriend?" I ask, heading over to the seat next to Zoey.

I wait for one of them to correct the label, but neither does. Liam just leans over the table, concentrating on the cue ball as Zoey flicks a glance at him, as if she's expecting something.

Ugh. They can't possibly be boyfriend-girlfriend this fast. Liam doesn't usually label the girls he churns through.

"I haven't even had a turn yet," Zoey says, once the awkward moment passes. "At least he never claimed to be a gentleman."

"We didn't bet," Liam says. "And it's not my fault I'm so good at this game."

"I want to play next," I say, dropping onto the chaise lounge in the corner and putting my feet up. They're pounding after a long afternoon working on my floor routine. After that one perfect pass a few days ago, I haven't nailed it since.

Liam sinks the last ball and Zoey stands up, pool cue in hand. "I'll play you, but I get to go first this time around." She walks to the side of the table.

Liam hands me his cue, mumbles something about a snack, and walks off, leaving the two of us alone.

Zoey racks the balls, arranging them and twirling them with such great care it's like they're made of glass. I watch, fascinated, as she narrows her eyes, assembling the balls in an odd diamond shape with the shiny black 8 is in the middle. I

70

don't know where the rest of the balls are, but we're at least a few short.

Then, carefully, she pulls the frame off and hangs it on the wall behind the table. "All set," she says, rounding to the far end, where she places the cue ball.

I want to ask her what game this is, since I've only ever played with a triangle-shaped mass of balls, but for some reason I don't want to ask. I'll look stupid.

I know a moment later, as the cue ball hits the tip of the diamond and the balls scatter with a loud *crack*, that she expected to win the game against my brother. And I know she's going to win this one. She sinks four balls before I get a chance to try at all.

She looks up at me, a triumphant, cocky grin on her face. "It's all yours."

I nod, circling the table and studying the balls. I'm just hoping to get one shot off without looking too dumb.

I lean over, staring down the cue ball for all I'm worth. Then I slide the stick back and let loose. The cue ball streaks across the table, smacking into a group of other balls.

The eight ball careens across the table, then drops into the corner pocket.

"Woohoo," I say, fist-pumping.

"You just lost," Zoey says. "And clearly you have no idea how to play pool."

"Oh." I glance back at the table. Obviously I should have inquired about the rules first. We've only had the table for six months, and I'm terrible at it since Liam never wants to play me.

"I'm going to go sit on the deck," I say. "You can come out if you want."

Outside, I stand at the railing, staring across the darkened waters at Brown's Point—still technically Tacoma, but the jagged edge of Puget Sound separates the two ends of town. Houses blaze light across the darkness, nothing more than tiny pricks of light in the distance.

Zoey doesn't follow. I don't even know if I want her to, but as I sit out here in the dark, listening to her laugh at something Liam must've said, I feel... lonely.

I don't know if it's how Ava is getting more wrapped up in Ayden lately, or how Liam's pulling away, or the fact that we haven't seen our parents in almost a month... But I can't seem to shake this shade of emptiness.

Ava and I used to connect on everything. We used to talk about our first crushes, our parents' fights, and everything in between.

I scowl out at the water. It makes me feel small. That's why I'm thinking these melancholy thoughts. I always feel introspective when I stare out at the bay.

"Contemplating your plans to solve world hunger?" Zoey says into the darkness.

I glance back, surprised she's come outside, with a glass in her hand that's filled with ice cubes and something dark.

"Something like that."

"Why don't you ever have friends over when I'm here?"

"Liam and I are friends."

"I mean, besides your brother."

"Ava's busy."

"Ava's seriously your only friend?" Zoey asks, and the surprise is evident in her voice.

"You already knew that," I say, "or you wouldn't have issued that little challenge."

"I mean, I knew you didn't have some enormous group of friends, but I figured you had more than Ava."

I feel my cheeks warm, and I hate it. "Why the hell do you care?"

That shuts her up for a second. Her lips press into a thin line. When she finally speaks, her voice is icy. "I'd rather have no friends than the artificial, backstabbing one you call a *best* friend."

"Oh, so that's what you're getting at. It's not about me at all, is it? You don't like Ava."

"Of course I don't like Ava. Don't be stupid."

"You don't even know her," I say, gripping the railing harder.

"Don't I? Go ask Ava about freshman year, then."

"She had nothing to do with that," I say, anger rising. "It was all you."

"She has *everything* to do with what everyone thinks of me," Zoey snaps. "An insult or two here and there, *fine*. But it's been a three-year smear campaign. Take your fucking blinders off and get a clue, will you?"

"They're not blinders," I say, my anger flashing to meet hers. "It's called loyalty. Maybe if you had some, you wouldn't be such a pariah in the first place."

"People were loyal to Hitler too, you know. It's not always a good quality."

I scowl and stare back out at the water, wondering why I'm even talking to her, and where the hell my brother went, and why she has such a chip on her shoulder, and…

"Ava's a good person," I say. "We both are. It's not my fault you two don't get along."

"You know, I thought you were smarter than that," Zoey says. "I thought you'd see through her bullshit eventually. But maybe you never will."

And she spins on her heel and stalks off, leaving me huddled there in the darkness.

ZOEY

I don't know why I'm doing this.

I don't owe Olivia Reynolds *anything*, most definitely not a birthday party, or whatever this is going to become.

The thing is, I can't get that image out of my head—of Olivia out on her deck alone in the darkness, staring out at the water, her shoulders slumped. The more I'm around her, the more I see this fragility about her, something a little cracked and broken behind the façade.

And I keep remembering what Liam said—that she's been clinging to him.

And now it's her birthday, and he's two hours away at the beach, and she's…she must be alone. I heard her, yesterday at school, telling Ava that she'd see her when she got back. I don't know where Ava's going, but it sure as hell sounds like out of town.

Which leaves one Olivia Reynolds alone on her birthday.

I grit my teeth, wondering why, for the millionth time, I've decided that Olivia needs me. She could probably rent some friends for the weekend.

"This will just take a second, okay?" I say, glancing over at Carolyn in the passenger seat.

"But I want to come with you," she whines. "*Pleeeeee-aaaaaaase?*"

I put my mom's battered old car in park and look up at the buildings that comprise Ruston Point.

"I'll only be a minute."

"But it looks so cool," she says, "and I want to ride in the elevator."

God, how pathetic is it that my sister, age ten, so rarely rides in elevators that it's a point of excitement?

"Fine. Come on. But don't say anything, okay? My friend might not even be home."

"Deal." She beams, jumping out of the car before I can change my mind.

I'm regretting the decision already, but I don't order her back into our dilapidated car. I simply walk to the front entry, pausing at the call box. I rake in an oddly shaky breath before I tap in *403*, and then, just as it starts to ring, I panic.

There was no call box on the wall inside their condo, like in all those old *Friends* episodes, so it's gotta be ringing someone's phone. I don't even know *where* it's ringing—their parents' phones, wherever the hell those would be, since their parents don't seem to be around much—or Liam's phone, or—

"Hello?"

Relief. It's Olivia. Maybe they have a house phone or something just for this purpose, or maybe it rings her cell.

"Um, hey, it's Zoey."

Silence. I glance over at Carolyn.

"Uh, Liam's out of town."

"I know. I was driving by on the way to the zoo with my little sister, and we passed your building. And then I just... I don't know, I turned around and thought I'd see if you wanted to come with us."

I press my finger to my lip in a *shhhh* sign when Carolyn opens her mouth to correct me. I hadn't driven past at all. I told Carolyn, when we left our place, that we were going to make a stop along the way.

"Oh."

"My mom got some free passes from her coworker. Three of them. So if you want to go..." My voice trails off because I don't know what else to say.

The box is silent, and I start to feel stupid. I shouldn't have invited her. I don't even know why I—

"Come on up. It'll take me a few minutes to get ready."

And then there's a buzz, and the door next to us clicks, and we're in.

I just invited Olivia Reynolds to go to the zoo with me and Carolyn, and I have no idea why.

———————

"Your car is much nicer than ours," Carolyn says from the back seat four hours later. I can't believe she's awake after so much running around, but maybe it's all the sugar. Olivia bought her soda and cotton candy, and she promptly consumed them both.

"Plus, ours makes funny noises," Carolyn adds.

I try not to cringe, instead pretending that I'm completely deaf. Oblivious. I mean, there were many reasons I asked Olivia if she could drive us to the zoo, and the funny noises topped the list.

"Um, thanks," Olivia says. "My dad let me pick it out."

"Awesome." Carolyn's voice is full of awe. "I would have picked something red."

"Yeah?" Olivia asks, glancing into the rearview mirror to meet my sister's eyes. At some point today, the two clicked. I'm almost envious. It's easy between them. Olivia doesn't have to do much to make Carolyn happy. She doesn't have to solve all the problems to make her forget that she still had that fading black eye. "My brother's car is red."

"You guys *both* have your own cars?"

"Mhmm."

I purse my lips and stare out the windshield, as if I can't even hear their conversation, as if I'm not thinking that Olivia has figured out how pathetically poor we are. I didn't miss the way she watched me as I moved my mom's car over to the guest parking space, with it coughing and hiccupping like it was on its last dying breath.

Hell, maybe it is. Maybe I'll get back in and it won't even start.

"That's so cool," Carolyn says. "I hope I get my own car someday."

"I'm sure you will." Olivia clicks on a blinker, turning and heading downhill toward their condo. "When I was a kid I used to want a motorcycle, just because my brother wanted one too. We'd smash cans on the top of our bike wheels so they'd grind against the tire and make sounds like a motorcycle."

"I don't have a bike, either," Carolyn says.

I squeeze my eyes shut and try not to notice the way the air went from happy and warm to dead cold.

"It got stolen," I say, opening my eyes again and glancing over at Olivia, trying to gauge her reaction.

Trying to gauge her pity level, really.

"Oh." She grips the steering wheel tighter but says nothing.

"It was too small, anyway," I add. "She'd had the same bike since, like, first grade."

"We have some of my older ones in our storage unit," Olivia offers. "There's one that will probably fit her. And it's red."

"It's fine," I say, my face warming. This is exactly what I don't want. From her. From Liam. From anyone. "You don't need to give us anything."

Carolyn's silent in the back seat, but I swear I can feel her hot gaze on the back of my neck. She wants a bike more than anything. She's had it on her Christmas list for two years.

"See, the thing is..." Olivia reaches over and taps the down button on her window, then sticks her hand out, letting it wave up and down in the wind. "My dad's been bugging the crap out of me to empty out the storage room for, like, months. If you take the bike, it would be one less thing I have to haul to Goodwill."

And then my seat kind of shakes as Carolyn grabs it. "Say yes, say yes, say yes."

I want to hang on to my protests, to deny Olivia the ability to give me anything, but faced with Carolyn's enthusiasm, my resistance dies away.

"Um, okay. Sure."

Olivia flashes me a smile, like she just single-handedly convinced General Lee to surrender in the Civil War. "Cool. Thanks for doing me a solid."

Right. She knows it's her who's granting the favor, making Carolyn happy.

"Sure," I say, going along with the farce.

"If you want to test it out," Olivia says, glancing back at Carolyn again, "we can use the big patio along the water. It's private for the residents."

"YES!" Carolyn says, bouncing up and down, kicking my seat. "Awesome."

Twenty minutes later, after Olivia goes into a storage unit somewhere in the labyrinth of their parking garage, Carolyn has her new bike.

Olivia and I sit on the stone ledge of a huge flower planter as Carolyn wobbles back and forth on the bike, gliding past us like a girl out of practice.

"Thank you," I say quietly, once she's out of earshot.

Olivia smiles at me, and when I look into her eyes, it's not pity or charity or anything like that. It's simply kindness.

"Sure. Any time." She watches Carolyn make another pass, and then adds quietly, "And thank you, too."

"For what?"

"For ensuring I didn't spend my birthday alone."

"It's not a big deal," I say.

"It is. You're the only one who cared. And I'm not even sure why. I haven't been very nice to you."

"I don't know. It just didn't seem fair. For you to be alone on your birthday, you know?"

"Yeah. Well, thanks."

"Sure."

"Do you want to work on our project once she gets tired of this?" Olivia asks, nodding toward Carolyn. "We can use my dad's office and she can watch movies on our big-screen in the den. We've got Netflix and cable and everything."

"That sounds great," I say. "My backpack's in the car. I made some notes earlier for what I want to cover."

"Cool. I'll watch your sister, if you want to go get them."

It's not until I walk away that I realize it's the first time anyone else has offered to watch Carolyn—the first time I've ever been able to walk away and know that she's safe.

OLIVIA

"I think your sister likes the surround-sound," I say as I step into the office space, where Zoey is already spreading out her notes.

"Oh yeah?" She doesn't looks up from her notes, just chews on her lips and says nothing else.

"Her eyes got big as saucers when the movie started." I grin. "We have a really cool popcorn maker, too. I flipped it on for her. Hope that's okay."

I still can't believe Zoey showed up today. Can't understand why she chose to rescue me from the downward spiral of my thoughts. Maybe she's not who I thought she was. Maybe there's more to her than the hard looks and the quasi-punk rock style.

"Oh, uh, yeah. Sure." She glances at me briefly, and it seems like something in her eyes has shifted. Like I've said the wrong thing.

"Something wrong?" I ask, pulling out a chair across the table from her.

"No. It's fine."

I narrow my eyes. "So then why do you sound so annoyed?"

Moments tick past, and neither of us speaks. I can just barely hear the low hum when the bass from Carolyn's movie hits. If I closed the door, we'd be sitting in silence.

"It's nothing," Zoey says. "Let's just work on our assignment."

"*Okaaaay*," I say, trying to figure out what's up with her mood flip. She seemed pretty happy twenty minutes ago, on the patio. "Um, let me see your notes."

"Why? They're not about a wealthy person," she says. "You probably can't relate."

I stare at her. "Jeez, what's your deal all of a sudden? Do I need to call off our BFFdom?"

Zoey slumps in her chair. "I'm sorry. I'm just in a mood. Seeing Carolyn here... how excited she was when she saw that big screen... you have no idea how much you have at your fingertips. How many things are just *handed* to you. If I didn't have to work at Burgerville all the time, if I didn't have to help with rent and utilities and think about a thousand things..."

Oh. That's what this is? "Look, I know we come from two different... backgrounds," I say. "But I can't change that."

"Whatever," she mutters under her breath, but her anger has clearly fizzled out. Now she just sounds resigned "Let's just work, okay?"

"Sure." The room falls silent and I stare at my empty

notebook. "Uh, were you really not going to let me see your notes, though? I'm not sure where to start."

"I didn't write them with anyone else in mind," she says. "They were for my eyes only."

I stare right at her, and she meets my gaze. And I get the feeling she's afraid to show me her papers. Like I'm going to laugh at them or judge them or something.

And it's the strangest thing, but as I stare back, I realize that I *want* Zoey to trust me, that it's suddenly the most important thing. I want her to see there's more to me than the things she keeps mocking. I want her to know that I know she's kept my secret—what little she saw of it—and I'm willing to keep all of hers.

Without breaking eye contact, she slowly lets go of the notebook and I slide it toward me.

The notes don't appear to be organized, and her writing is frenetic, angled, scribbled in haste. Like she was taking notes about a movie without taking her eyes off the screen.

Dawn to Dusk. Research working environment—hot like Burgerville? First Aid kits?

Hierarchy—supervisors also lower class like Rita is at Burgerville? Is that what they are destined for in 1790, too— no ability to claw up? Lower class for life?

Any way to escape future—opportunities? Or are they stuck like me?

RESPECT—any from upper class? Or are they all like Olivia?

I swallow as I keep scanning the notes. This one page is like seeing her innermost thoughts.

It's like seeing how she sees herself. The down-trodden, the trapped, the stepped on.

"I just got an idea," I say.

"And?"

"Instead of writing our parts as factual essays, we should write a fictional account from two people."

"Like, a short story?"

"Yeah. And our characters should know each other," I say.

"Why would they know each other?"

"Because the factory where your character works is owned by my character's family," I say, for some reason getting excited. "So my character can visit the factory, and she'll actually see your character working."

"And mine would see your character, too..." Zoey says, her voice trailing off.

"Exactly," I say. "So not only do we, as writers, compare and contrast the characters, but they'll see the differences between them themselves."

"And we could alternate the narrative. Start big picture, the basics of their day. The luxuries or lack thereof," Zoey says, warming to the idea. "And then once they actually get to the factory, they'll see each other from afar, and make assumptions about one another. And then we'll slowly boil it down, from those first impressions to the dreams and desires of women back then."

I grin. "Exactly. Almost like a feminist approach to everyday life—these two girls, trapped by who they are, taking control of their own lives. We could cover a single, fictional day, going back and forth between their points of view, ultimately building toward the moment when they realize they have more in common than they ever thought."

She sits back in her chair, staring at me like she can't believe I thought that up. "I like it."

"I thought you would," I say, pushing her notebook back toward her. "It'll delve much deeper than what we'd originally thought. The papers will no longer stand alone as comparisons; they'll be pretty intertwined."

"Then I guess you'd better quit slacking and start putting together some notes."

"I will. But this is going to take more collaboration. You know that, right?" I say.

"You start brainstorming, and I'll write my first scene and email it to you," Zoey says. "If you think it works, you add yours and send it back. Each scene should just be a couple of pages, and we'll each have to write one every other day, to keep it moving and finish on time."

"Okay." I dig a pen out of the front pocket of my backpack. "Here's my email address. Once you send me your scene, we'll go from there." Just as I finish writing the dot com part, I glance up at her and scribble down a little more. "And my cell number. In case we need to get together, or you want to ask about my character."

"Okay," Zoey says. "I'll get it to you tomorrow, after my shift."

"Ugh, you have to work on Sunday? *Again?*"

She nods. "I don't always, but one of my coworkers talked me into swapping."

"Oh. Okay, well, I'll start brainstorming."

"Sounds good," Zoey says. "Anyway, I should probably get back home so my mom can use the car."

"Sure you don't want to let your sister finish the movie?"

"Some other time, maybe?"

"Yeah. Totally."

Ten minutes later, I'm in the office alone, scribbling down notes. My pen flies across the page, word after word, idea after idea.

It's easy to think of all the ways my character would be different than hers.

ZOEY

Olivia's been on my mind all day while I clean the stupid fryers and run the tomato slicer and sweep the floors, all things that have nothing to do with her.

The mere idea of Olivia herself doing such chores, actually, brings a funny picture to mind. I bet she could rock the visor, though.

The thing is, there was something in that look she gave me when she said she wanted to read my notes. It was this long, lingering gaze that I could practically *feel*, like a heavy blanket draping over me. In that one crazy moment, I would have given her whatever she wanted, my notes included.

She probably uses that look a lot to get what she wants. She could use it on teachers and boys and daddy dearest.

And so I let her see my notebook. I let her read my unfiltered thoughts, the things I'd been scribbling down at Burgerville the day before. The despair and the frustration as

I watched the minutes of my break tick away, as I smelled the grease leaching into my clothes, as I listened to the horrible pop music crackling through the overhead speakers.

I'd braced myself for some kind of uncomfortable laugh. For her to look up and smile and shove it back at me with a look that said she felt sorry for me.

But the strangest thing happened instead.

It was like she understood me. Like she knew exactly how I'd felt as I scribbled those things down.

And her new idea for the project is genius. It's just too bad I have to stay up late tonight to finish it. All I really want is to crawl into bed.

I shove a bag of fries and unsold burgers into my backpack. Carolyn won't be awake, but she's not opposed to eating reheated fast-food for breakfast, so I'm not about to let them go to waste.

I'm the last out the door tonight, just like on a lot of other nights. No one likes the closing shift because of all the cleaning, so I get it more often than others.

After zipping up my jacket, I pull my backpack over my shoulders and walk over to the alarm. I glance outside for the first time in more than half an hour—it took that long to wipe everything down and mop—and my heart sinks.

It's pouring.

I pull my hood over my head, punch in the code, and hit *arm*. And then I dash out onto the sidewalk, locking the door behind me.

The sky's a dark, angry black. There's no way this storm is going to let up any time soon. I'll just have to move quickly and dream of the hot shower I'll take when I get home. I can't get that soaked in just a mile, right?

Just as I step into the rain, a sleek silver car pulls into the parking lot. Between the tinted windows and the raindrops, it's impossible to see inside.

It looks familiar. It looks…

Like Olivia's car.

It pulls up beside me at the curb and the window glides down. "Get in," Olivia says, hitting the unlock button.

I don't say a word, just round the car and climb into the passenger seat. As the door slams shut and the rain drips from my hair, into my eyes, I realize how wet I am just from dashing around the car.

"Uh, sorry about the water," I say, trying not to lean back too far and let my wet jacket touch the seats.

"Don't worry about it. The leather holds up to just about anything," Olivia says, putting her window back up. "Liam puked in the back seat once."

I cringe and glance back.

"I had it detailed," she says. "Made him pay for it."

"Oh."

She doesn't put the car in drive right away. "Were you really going to walk in this?"

"No, I have a Pegasus around back," I say. "I tied it up by the dumpster."

She snorts. "I'm being serious."

"I was there, wasn't I? And do you see a car sitting around waiting for me?"

"Where's your mom?" she asks.

"Busy," I say. She's probably just watching TV, but to pick me up, she'd have to get Carolyn out of bed, and I'd never want her to do that.

"Oh. Uh, so tell me which way to go."

"South on Division."

She puts the car into gear and heads out of the parking lot, gliding smoothly onto the street.

"Why are you here?" I ask. "Because, um, you didn't have to do this for me."

"I know. And besides, I was being kinda self-serving. You need to get your scene done. I want a good grade in the class."

"Afraid your perfect 4.0 could get marred?"

She glances at me out of the corner of her eye. "I have a 2.7."

"You do not," I say, my mouth dropping.

"I do. I'm not actually that smart, you know. I struggle to pull Bs, and then math drags it down from there. And I just bombed another test. This assignment is important, which makes you, by extension, important."

"Huh," I say, leaning back in the seat as I watch the windshield wipers fly back and forth and back and forth. "So I finally discovered one tiny thing about you that's not perfect."

"I'd see being a bitch as a pretty big personality flaw," Olivia says.

I stifle a laugh, glancing over at her to figure out whether she's being serious or just mocking what I said about her.

"I mean, sometimes you're actually pretty nice," I say.

"Thanks." A smile plays at Olivia's lips. The way the street lamps and the passing headlights illuminate her, she looks kind of beautiful. For once, she's looking at me with respect and it seems so genuine.

Olivia and genuine are not two words I've ever thought together in one sentence.

"Do you work this late every night?"

"No," I say. "Nobody really works full time, so they can avoid paying benefits."

"That's something you should talk about," she says.

"Benefits? No one at Burgerville is going to get benefits. It's practically part of their business plan."

"Yeah, no, that's not what I meant. I meant in the assignment. There probably weren't any benefits back then, either. No paid time off or health care."

"Right. So I guess things haven't changed much in a hundred years," I say.

"I mean, some stuff has changed. You *are* in a BMW 3 Series. With the flick of a button, your butt can be warmed," she says, tapping something on the dash. "Also you're totally fogging it up in here." She flips on the air, blasting it at the windshield.

"Sorry," I say. "And thanks. I don't think I've said that. Thank you for the ride."

"You have my number now. You can always text if you need one."

"Yeah, maybe," I say. "Take a left up here."

Olivia puts on her blinker, and for a while, the rhythmic clicking is the only sound in the darkness. We glide around the corner, and tiny square houses pop up on either side of the car.

"I've never been down this road," she says. And then she squeezes her lips together as if realizing how insulting it was to say that. Of course she hasn't been down this road. Her kind don't have any reason to be down this road.

"Pretty trees," she says, as if to make up for pointing out our differences.

She's trying to be ... nice. What a weird thing. I'm riding in Olivia Reynolds's BMW and she's trying not to hurt my feelings.

"Yeah, I planted them myself," I say.

"Really?"

"No." I laugh. "God, they're probably like thirty or forty years old."

"Oh. Right."

"Why are you doing this, really?" I ask, turning away so I don't have to look her in the eyes.

"To repay you. For the zoo."

"You didn't have to do that. It wasn't a favor to be repaid."

"I know. But it meant a lot to me."

"Okay," I say, leaning my head back against the seat. "As long as I'm not your project."

"Project?"

"You know, charity case. Project. I don't need you sweeping in and picking me up, or giving my sister your old stuff."

"Right. Sure. I mean, I don't really see you like that. So it's not a big deal."

"Really?"

Olivia laughs. "This is why you don't have friends, Zoey.

You're too suspicious. Sometimes people can just be nice, you know."

"I guess."

The car falls silent for a while, the only sounds coming from the wipers as they whip back and forth. Then Olivia crinkles her nose up. "You smell like French fries."

"I have a to-go bag in my backpack. I get a free meal after every shift." I sigh, as quietly as possible, as I watch the rain stream down the passenger window. I reach up and paint a zigzag in the fog with my finger.

"Go left on Stewart," I say. "My house is the third one on the right."

And then I brace myself for her reaction when she sees it.

OLIVIA

Her house is hideous.

I can tell she's embarrassed by how fast she grabs her bag and shoves the car door open. I try to focus my eyes on her and not the crumbling structure behind her, try to act like I don't even notice it, but it's hard not to.

I can't believe it's even livable.

"Uh, thanks again," she says, leaning over, one hand still on the door. "For the ride."

"I mean, I didn't want you to melt."

Her nose crinkles up. "I'm not the wicked witch."

I grin. "I meant like sugar, because you're so sweet?"

"Right." Zoey laughs. "Whatever. See you later, okay?"

She slams the door a little too hard and then rushes across the lawn. I wait, watching, until she shoves her way inside and the door shuts behind her.

Right then. Time to go home.

I turn around in an adjacent driveway and then head back the way I came. Our homes aren't that far apart by car, but it would be a long walk. And while I'm not positive, I'm pretty sure she must have walked home that first time Liam brought her over. I don't remember him leaving at all, but Zoey left at some point.

I leave the radio off as I pass by dozens of darkened houses, some of them boarded up. My thoughts swim in and out.

There's something enigmatic about Zoey. She's like a puzzle where the pieces don't fit. One minute she's angry and lashing out and another, like that moment when I took her notebook, she's vulnerable. She'd hate it if I said that. I know her well enough to know that about her, anyway, even if I haven't quite figured out what she's all about.

Soon the houses get bigger, the paint gets brighter, the windows get larger. And then I'm rounding the bend and pulling onto Ruston Way, gliding up to our condo building.

A short elevator ride later and I'm inside our place, which is as dark as the streets I just finished driving.

"Liam?" I call out, my voice booming in the space. "Hello?"

He's gotta be home from the beach by now. We have class in the morning.

I flick on a light, and he leaps up so fast I screech and jump backward, slamming into the wall.

"SURPRISE!" he screams, throwing his arms up.

"Jesus, you scared the hell out of me," I say, my eyes sweeping over the thing in his hand.

A present. It's a little box, wrapped in silver paper with a pink bow.

He gives me a toothy grin. "Sorry. I heard you coming and couldn't resist."

"Next time try harder," I say. "What's that?"

He steps forward, holding the box out. "For you. Happy birthday."

"I didn't get you anything." I figured if he wasn't even going to *see me* on our birthday, we were skipping the presents, too.

"That's okay."

I accept the tiny box, slipping my finger under the wrapping paper.

"I'm sorry," he says.

I glance up. "Uh, for what?"

"For ditching you. For breaking tradition. I felt kind of bad once I was at the casino."

"Why, did you lose all your money and have a miserable time?"

Liam pulls out a stool and sits, leaning forward and resting his elbows on the counter. "No. It was fun. It just wasn't... it wasn't quite right without you."

"Oh." Some little part of my heart heals, hearing that. Like maybe he's not totally over hanging out with me, even if I am his tag-a-long sister.

I rip off the wrapping paper and find a little white box. When I slide off the lid, a silver bracelet stares back at me. It's a chain of little starfish. I know without asking that he bought it in the casino gift shop; he didn't go out of his way for me, but it doesn't matter. He thought about me. "It's pretty," I say.

"You think?"

I look up at him, realizing he's perched on the edge of the stool waiting for my response. I guess he does actually feel bad.

I sigh. "Yeah. Thank you. And I *guess* I can forgive you."

"Really?"

"But you still owe me one," I say.

"Why don't we go to the cabin next weekend, then? We could leave right after school on Friday and do two nights there, like you wanted."

"Really?" I say.

"Yeah. Let's do it. It's a week late, but it'll still be fun. We can't break our tradition."

I smile, relief barreling through me. "Okay. I'm in."

ZOEY

I take the elevator up to Olivia's condo, straightening my shirt and grimacing when I see a little grease stain. I'm just raising my fist to the front door when it swings open.

"Oh, uh, hi," I say, staring right at Liam. He's not the one who buzzed me in—Olivia is. It didn't even occur to me that he'd be home.

"This is a pleasant surprise," he says. "I wasn't expecting you."

"Actually," I say, suddenly feeling awkward, "Olivia and I have a project together. I came here to work on it."

"Oh." Liam's voice falls.

"Why do you sound so bummed?" I say, poking him in the stomach. "Your other date cancel on you?"

He steps back and motions me into the house. "I haven't gone out with anyone else since we met at the gas station."

I blink. When he'd casually called me his girlfriend last

week, I thought it was just part of his flirty nature. Like I was "his girl" but not his *exclusive* girl.

"You're kidding, right?" I step into the entry, kicking off my worn-out sneakers.

"Nah. You're basically cooler than everyone else, so there's no point."

I swallow and ignore the tightening in my chest, unsure of whether I'm pleased or panicked. Both. Definitely both. Liam is actually *choosing* me. Surreal. Freshman-year Zoey would have totally peed her pants in excitement over something like this.

I stand in the entryway, not sure if it would be weird to just walk away from him right now after a proclamation like that.

Before I can decide what to say, Liam speaks again. "Uh, so do you want to come with us to our lake house this weekend?"

I raise a brow. "You guys have a lake house? Why, is the Puget Sound condo not enough?"

He stops in front of me, running his hands up and down my arms and staring into my eyes. "No, this is home. The lake house is more like a cabin. We go every year in the fall, and I'm hereby inviting you."

"Oh. Just us?"

He shrugs. "I got my fill of my friends last weekend, but Olivia will probably invite someone."

"Oh," I say, my voice falling. A whole weekend with Liam and Olivia I could handle, but not if Ava is there too. "I don't know—"

"You won't have to hang out with Olivia and her friends. I don't. The cabin has two levels. They usually stay downstairs."

The way he's facing me, his hands squeezing my arms, is intense.

I swallow. "Um, maybe. I'll think about it, okay?"

"Please? You're the only one I'm asking." He pauses, studying me. "And the only one I really want to go."

My heart spasms. I can't say no to him when he's looking at me like that and being so serious, so heartfelt, for the first time in ... well, probably ever. I hardly know this version of Liam. "Oh. Yeah, okay. I'll go."

"Awesome. I can't wait." He wraps his arms around me, picking me up and spinning me around before setting me down again and brushing his lips against mine. His fingers graze my chin as he tips my head back, and I close my eyes, enjoying the kiss.

"Me neither," I say when he pulls away. I'm not quite sure when this happened, when we became two people who can casually kiss in the entryway of his condo in the middle of the day. That same panic and pleasure spins through me. I'm not sure what to make of the idea of something ... *real* with Liam.

I thought we were just having fun. Now it's going to be something?

"Hey, Zoey," Olivia's voice calls. I turn to see her standing in the hall. I don't miss the way her gaze flits over the spots where Liam and I are touching. The way his hand is on my lower back, pulling me toward him, making me sort of arch my back. I feel like I just got caught by my mom or something. It's...awkward.

"Hey," I reply, pulling away from him.

"So, ready to work?"

I nod, parting ways with Liam and following her into her dad's office.

"You can use the desktop if you want," she says, plunking down on a little fainting couch or chaise or whatever they're called. She turns so that she's leaning against the backrest, facing the desk. She crosses her legs at the ankles and rests the computer on her lap.

"Okay, yeah." I go to the leather desk chair, turning it around so that I can sit. I feel like the president or something behind such a stately desk, in a chair with big arm rests and a tall back.

I wiggle the mouse and the computer comes to life. My word document is already open on the screen.

"I pulled it off my email for you," Olivia explains. "And I added my latest scene. I still need to finish it, so don't like, get all nitpicky or anything, but it should give you an idea what I'm thinking."

"Oh. Thanks." I scroll to the bottom, to where my last section ends and hers begins. Her character's name is Priscilla, and it doesn't take long to fall into her point of view.

Priscilla stood behind the window in the second-floor office, looking out across the massive expanse of the warehouse. This was the view her father loved. This was where he always stood, his chest puffed out as if he were the ruler of a kingdom he'd built, brick by brick.

But Priscilla knew that it was not his sweat that built the warehouse. It was not his callused, bloody hands that put this place together, piece by piece.

It was his money.

Below, the machines hummed, a never-ending racket barely muffled by the glass and the walls. On the floor, she knew, the machinery was even louder.

Deafening.

She watched as a girl—someone close to her own sixteen years of age—scurried across the floor, dodging and spinning around the other workers in her haste to carry whatever was in a large crate to its intended destination. There was a beautiful grace to the way she moved, even with her shoulders hunched, her arms laden down with heavy materials.

Almost as if she could feel Priscilla's gaze, the girl looked up.

And they locked eyes.

Moments later, the shift whistle screeched. It made Priscilla jump and break eye contact with the girl. When she blinked and looked again, the girl was gone.

"This is good," I say. "It's the moment our characters meet."

"Obviously," Olivia says, laughing.

"I mean, we've done all this lead-up to it. The morning routines and the housing and the family, and then we finally get to the warehouse and it's an important moment. You wrote it well."

"So, I was thinking," Olivia says, sitting up. "My character would keep thinking about your character. Long after they part ways. She's seen something in her eyes, and it's going to haunt her until they can meet again."

There's something...intense about the look Olivia is giving me, like she's trying to convey some hidden subtext.

Okay," I say, swallowing.

"So I thought maybe what you would write is what your character thinks of my character after they each go their own way, you know? Since this moment was from my character's point of view. You can show that these girls have a really deep connection. Something other people might not, you know, understand, since they seem so different."

It's suddenly hard to breathe. I nod and stare at the monitor to avoid looking at Olivia. "Sure. Yeah, I can do that."

"So what will you write?"

I pick up a pen from the cup next to the monitor, mostly to give me something to do with my hands, and then reach for a yellow notepad. "Uh," I say. I was thinking, maybe..." My voice trails off. "She's jealous."

"She is?"

"She sees your character up there in the window, out of the dust and the sounds—protected, I guess—and she wishes she were her."

"Why?"

"Because she assumes your character has it easy. That your character will never know the hurt and the heartache and the hard life."

The room falls silent and I force my eyes to remain on the notebook.

"What's going on with you and my brother?" Olivia says.

I jerk my head up and look over at her. "Change of subject, much?"

"Just wondering."

"I've told you before," I say, staring at the notepad again. What's with her sudden fascination with my relationship with Liam? "I'm more of a happy-for-now kind of girl. We're having fun. He's a cool guy."

"He doesn't usually 'have fun' with the same girl for more than a week or two. And he didn't object when I referred to you as his girlfriend."

I glance over at her. "Then it's him you should be questioning."

She stares at me dead-on, chewing on her bottom lip. "Are you? His girlfriend? I mean, are you really into him like that?"

I raise a brow. "Last I checked, neither of us was writing our wedding vows, so…"

Olivia leans back and pulls her feet up onto the chaise. "Whatever. I was just curious, is all. You two looked pretty cozy in the hall earlier."

I make a non-committal humming sound.

"Anyway. So for my next scene, I was thinking…"

But as I listen to her drone on and on about her plans for the rest of her scene, I can't get her questions out of my head.

Why does she care that I'm with Liam?

OLIVIA

I'm pretty much folded in half in the back seat, staring at the place where Liam's hand rests on Zoey's knee and trying to decide why it is that it looks so...

Wrong.

It's a very couple-y thing to do. That's what's wrong with it. Liam isn't supposed to connect with the same girl long enough to become a real couple with her. He's supposed to get infatuated for three point five seconds, move on, and hang out with me again.

When Liam pulls off the county two-lane highway onto the bumpy, curving, narrow road leading to our cabin, Zoey sits up straighter, staring out the window. "This isn't what I was picturing," she says. "I mean, I know you said it was a cabin, but..."

Liam flashes her a grin. "You thought it would be like our condo, huh?"

She nods, taking in the tiny roofs half-covered in pine needles and the flashes of the small, quiet lake between the trees.

"Our mom's family owned it before she met my dad," I say, relaxing against the seat.

"Dad's the side with money," Liam adds. "My grandpa— my mom's dad—bought this place decades ago, when it was basically a shell, and rebuilt it with his own hands."

"Oh."

Zoey glances back at me, her smile wide and brilliant, and then suddenly I get it.

She's happy we're taking her to an old family cabin, something more in her comfort zone than our pricey condo.

Liam slows next to a sign that says *Remein*, and then coasts down an angled driveway, pulling to a stop next to a small wooden cabin with a green roof.

"So," I say, sitting up and unfastening my seat belt, "I'm guessing Liam didn't inform you of the lack of plumbing?"

She flicks a glance back at me, clearly expecting to see that I'm joking. "Um, no."

"There's an outhouse," Liam interjects. "And we've got one of those big bottled water dispenser things for drinking."

"Oh." Yeah, definitely not what Zoey had expected, based on the way she looks like she's trying not to cringe. "Does it at least have electricity?"

I snicker. "Yes. We didn't go back in time or anything. But my mom refuses to let my dad upgrade this place. She said she grew up out here, every summer. She wants it to feel like it always did."

"That's kind of nice," Zoey says, unbuckling. "Sentimental, you know?"

"Come on in. It's not as bad as it sounds," I say.

We climb out and go around to the back of the car, grabbing our backpacks as Liam lifts the cooler from the trunk. He uses a key on his ring to open the back door, and then it swings inward with a loud creak. "Welcome to your humble abode for the weekend."

"Lay off the cheese," I say, pushing past him.

"Don't mind my snarly sister," I hear him say to Zoey. "She's just bummed she has to sleep downstairs alone. But it's not my fault her friends are so lame."

I flip him off over my shoulder, then head out the back door to take the outdoor steps to the basement, where I'll be staying this weekend. I shove the slider open, then walk into the basement and toss my bag onto one of the twin beds.

There are four beds in here, actually, which makes it painfully obvious I'm alone. Ava made some half-hearted promise about how maybe she could come out on Sunday, after some big gala she's going to with her parents is over, but I know it was an empty promise.

She's not coming.

While my brother bunks with Zoey. They'll be in the bedroom right over my own.

God, I'd wanted to badly to come here for our birthday, but now that we're here, I just want to go home again. I don't know if I can sit around all weekend watching Liam be lovey-dovey and happy with her while I'm just...down here. Alone. Staring at the walls, or the lake, or whatever.

I scowl, reaching for the little pocket at the front of my bag, where I find my little purple box.

I swallow a Xanax, washing it down with a swig of water.

Maybe once it kicks in, I won't care that this weekend is going to suck.

ZOEY

I'm standing in the middle of a narrow, galley-style kitchen; the sink has no faucet. I wonder how it is that this cabin turned out to be nothing like I'd imagined.

"For washing dishes," Liam says, gesturing to the sink. "Using the bottled water, of course. Don't go too crazy dumping pop or anything like that into the sink—it just drains into a pipe that leads outside."

I nod, following him deeper into the cabin and then realizing that there isn't much farther to go.

A small living room to the left, a kitchen table on the right, and a big window up ahead.

I walk to it, peering out at the prettiest, most pristine lake I've ever seen. The surface is like glass. Across the way, other small cabins nestle amongst the trees. Below, a small shed sits near the edge of the water and a dock stretches out, a little rowboat tied up to the end.

"It's pretty," I say, staring out the window and feeling the tightness in my chest unwind. This is a place I can relax. A place where I can enjoy the weekend. Suddenly, as the next forty-eight hours stretch out in front of me, I'm happy Liam convinced me to come.

"Yeah. I think so. Come on, you can put your backpack in the bedroom." He tugs my hand and I follow him away from the window, through the doorway at the edge of the living room. A small room is tucked away, a king-sized bed taking up most of the space.

Until this moment, I hadn't actually thought about where I would sleep—or that he'd expect me to sleep with him. That fact is apparent as we set our bags down next to each other.

Liam has been … amazing so far. But I just met him two weeks ago. All we've done is kiss a couple of times. Now I don't know what to think, what he expects, and the peace I felt as I stared out the window melds into knots of worry.

It's not that I expect him to force the issue or anything.

"Where's Olivia sleeping?" I ask.

"Downstairs. There's a basement. You can't access it from inside; you have to go through the slider outside."

"Oh." So we're really going to be alone. In a bed. Together. Right.

He takes off his fancy silver watch, setting it down on the table beside the bed. I wonder if he did that because time doesn't really matter, here. "Anyway, do you want to take the rowboat out?"

"Like to go fishing?"

"Nah. I mean, we could fish if you want to, but I don't

really have the patience." He grins. "I'd just like to row around the lake for a bit."

"Oh. Sure. Yeah, that sounds fun."

"Cool. I'll get the oars and life jackets, if you want to go tell Olivia. She can come, if she feels like it."

"Sure."

I leave the little bedroom behind and find my way to a door that leads onto the deck at the back of the cabin. The view is even better out here, totally unobstructed. The railing is white iron around the edges, but in the middle, it's just huge plates of glass. I breathe deeply, raking in the scent of pine and fresh air.

And I can't help the smile. I would've asked about inviting Carolyn if I'd known it would be like this. She'd love this place.

There's always next time.

I blink, surprised by the thought. Next time? Do I expect to be with Liam long enough for there to be a next time?

Or do I think of Olivia as an actual friend, and that she might invite me herself?

I shake my head, forcing myself to concentrate on this weekend and not the future as I head to the steps, still training my eyes on the lake. It's stunning. The reflection of the trees glimmers on the water as I descend the staircase and find my way around the corner, to where another set of windows faces the lake and a sliding glass door is already half-open.

"Olivia?" I call, stepping through the door.

The basement is one big room, with just a couple old

bunk beds on the far wall and two twin beds in the middle, between the posts that must support the structure.

"This looks like a little kid's slumber party dream," I say when my eyes finally land on Olivia, who's sprawled out on one of the single beds.

"It was," Olivia replies, smiling as she looks up at me. "Ava and I used to stay up all night and listen to the radio and eat junk food. It was awesome."

I nod.

"Can I tell you something?" she says a moment later.

"Sure."

"It's just . . . you kind of freak me out."

I stand there, half in the cabin and half out, my heart pounding in my ears.

"What do you mean?"

"I'd tell you if I knew," she says.

"Oh."

Olivia doesn't say anything more, and I start to feel like an idiot for just standing there, the warm autumn air mixing with the cooler temps of the basement. So I step back outside the cabin. "Uh, me and Liam are going for a boat ride if you want to go."

"Nah, you go ahead. I feel like a nap."

"Okay." I stand there for a moment longer, waiting for her to sit up and say something else, but she doesn't. She just lies there unmoving, staring at the ceiling. "Uh, see you later."

The lake is perfect. I'm sitting at the front of the boat, on top of a couple of those floating cushions that double as life preservers, letting my fingertips skim the water as Liam rows. I feel kind of silly making him do all the work, but he insisted, and now I'm glad he did.

I stare up at the blue sky as the sun tucks behind a puffy white cloud. "It's nice out here."

"I think so."

I let my fingers dip lower, the lake water splashing up against my palm.

"Does Olivia like it?" I ask. "I always pictured her as more of a five-star-resort type. Like her ideal vacation is someplace with a spa attached."

"Actually, she's always loved coming here. When we were little she convinced our mom to have Christmas here."

"Really?" I glance over at him, blinking against the residual effects of the bright skyline.

"Yeah," he says, chuckling at the memory. The warmth of his smile makes me smile back. "Dad hated the idea, but Olivia convinced Mom. The cabin holds a lot of fond memories for her, too. Her dad died years ago, but she spent a lot of time with him here, helping him fix it up, you know? So we all came out here on Christmas Eve."

"That sounds amazing."

"It was a lot better in theory than in practice. Mom had such a hard time making Christmas dinner without plumbing. And I heard Dad in the middle of the night, leaving in the big SUV."

"He didn't like it?"

"No, he had to drive back to our house for all the presents," he says, cracking a big smile. "There hadn't been enough room for them with all of us and the suitcases and everything."

I laugh. "Aww. That's a long drive. How nice of him."

"It was," Liam says, getting a wistful sort of tone. "They used to be around more, you know? Even last year wasn't this bad. They'd be home most weekends, and even the weekday trips were only a few nights. I guess they figured Olivia and I are old enough to handle things on our own."

"You only *just* turned eighteen," I say, leaning back against my makeshift chair again, my fingertips dipping back into the water.

"My dad sold his first company when he was seventeen."

"Really? What was it?"

"I don't know. Something to do with cardboard. Some kind of new design to make stronger boxes with less material."

"Hmm. I suddenly feel like a slacker."

He kicks my foot and I look up. "You're so not a slacker. You work all those shifts and you get good grades."

"I know," I say, surprised by the compliment. Apparently easy-breezy Liam actually pays attention. "I was kidding."

"Does it suck?" he asks.

"Does what suck?"

"Having to work so much. Juggling everything."

"Oh. Yeah, I mean … yeah. Sometimes it's really tiring."

"It must be."

It's weird, this conversation. The honesty, the depth to

it. It's the first time he's really asked me any probing questions about myself, or shared any of his thoughts.

We fall silent for a while, and I close my eyes to concentrate on the quiet splashing of the oars hitting the water, the coolness of the lake on my skin. I think I fall asleep at some point, because a moment later I wake to a bump and realize we've knocked up against something, and a shadow falls over me. I pop open my eyes to discover I'm sitting in the shadow of the dock. I sit up as Liam ties a rope to one of the cleats, looping it around and around and around. Then he reaches back and helps me stand, and we climb out of the boat.

I'm reluctant to leave it behind. But it would be silly to climb back in, so I follow him back to the cabin.

OLIVIA

I'm sitting on the creaky old couch in the living room when I hear them down at the dock, their laughter and voices drifting up through the open window. I quickly reach over and turn on the radio, so it's not like I'm sitting here alone, and grab one of the years-old *Good Housekeeping* magazines off the coffee table.

They breeze through the door a moment later. Liam's mumbling something that makes Zoey giggle, and she leans over, resting a hand on his arm.

Something streaks though me as I watch her fingers curl around his biceps.

Jealousy.

I blink. I've never been jealous of Liam. Maybe he has someone at the cabin with him, unlike me, but I'm not going to start getting jealous of him now.

I toss the magazine back onto the coffee table and hope

they don't notice how old and stupid it is. "How was the tour of the lake?"

"Awesome," Zoey says, beaming. "It's way bigger than it looks from the dock."

Liam made her smile, from ear to ear.

The streak of jealousy grows a mile wide. I've never seen her smile quite like that, so naturally. And for some stupid reason the urge to make her do it again is almost overwhelming.

"You should see it at night," I find myself saying. "With the stars."

"That sounds cool," she says, glancing over at Liam.

He puts his hands up in a surrender pose. "Don't look at me, I'm going to drink beer. You know the rules."

I raise my hand up like a boy scout pledge. "Thou shalt not mix alcohol and boating, lest you be struck dead by God."

He rolls his eyes. "I don't think Mom said it quite like that."

I shrug. "I'll take you later," I say to Zoey. "It's way too pretty to miss for a beer."

And she beams again, making it all worth it.

———

We're sitting on canvas camping chairs surrounding the rusted iron campfire pit. The fire crackles and pops, sparks lifting into the air with the smoke.

"I can't believe you've never had a banana boat," Liam is saying.

"I've never even heard of it."

"S'mores?"

Zoey laughs. "Yes, I've had freaking s'mores. And not just the Pop-Tarts ones."

Watching her poke his side, her teeth glinting in the moonlight when she lets back a laugh, is so surreal I'm hardly talking.

Zoey is different here. That advice I gave her, telling her to put down her guard and give people a chance—turns out she's someone else when she's away from it all.

When she's with Liam.

She laughs and lets loose. And yeah, she's taken a few sips of his beer, but not enough to make this a product of drinking.

It tastes bitter, this realization that Liam's here and happy and getting Zoey to loosen up, but she doesn't act like this for me.

"Well, prepare for deliciousness," Liam says, his tone serious. "These will blow your mind."

"Is it bad if I admit I'm not a huge fan of bananas?" she asks.

"What! Blaspheme!"

She laughs again, watching as he pulls the tinfoil out of the fire.

"Besides," my brother says, "it doesn't really matter because it's not really about the bananas. You could put marshmallows and chocolate on a saltine and it would make it taste like heaven."

He holds the foil by the edges, pinching it between his

fingers just long enough to drop it onto the little camping table between me and Zoey. "Give it a second to cool, or you'll burn your hands *and* your mouth."

"And then how would I flip burgers?" she says. "That would be a real travesty."

I don't know why it's rubbing me the wrong way, her joking around, being all playful with him, but I've reached my limit. "You didn't make me one," I say to my brother, even though I noticed this twenty minutes ago.

He glances up at me as if surprised, the dancing flames casting shadows on his face. "That's because it's BYOB. Bring your own banana. You were supposed to bring it down from upstairs. I only grabbed two."

"It's fine," I say, standing, trying to keep the frustration and jealousy from my voice. "Don't worry about it."

And then I get up and walk away.

I hear Liam murmur something to Zoey under his breath, and fight the urge to whirl around and glare at him. He's not worth it. They're not worth it. They can sit out here and be all cutesy or whatever. I don't need them.

I got to the basement and dig out my backpack, searching for my little pillbox again. I can't remember where I put it earlier, and that dose didn't seem to have been enough because I can feel everything inside me coiling tighter and tighter. I need another pill.

Before I can locate the box, the door behind me slides open. I turn around to see Zoey walking in, paper plate in her hand. "I cut it in half," she says, holding up the plate.

"It's fine," I say, waving her away as I zip my bag up.

The pill will have to wait. "You can have it." I try to ignore the strange warmth I feel as she sits at the foot of the bed.

Gratefulness. That's what it is. This realization that at least Zoey cares about me enough to give up half a banana boat.

"Don't be silly." She picks up one half and then slides the plate toward me.

I stare down at it. I probably shouldn't eat it. I skipped all those meals for a reason. But as Zoey licks gooey chocolate off her finger, I give in. I sit down, so that we're side by side, and place the plate on my lap.

"Thanks," I say, picking up the extra fork she brought me.

"You're welcome."

The sounds of Liam's stereo and the crackling fire drift in through the open window, but inside it's silent as we eat our treats.

It's the best-tasting banana boat I've ever had. Warm, squishy banana, and ooey gooey chocolate and marshmallow. Neither of us speak until I've had the last bite, and I ball the tin foil up.

"Should we take the boat out now?" I say finally. Whatever fit of annoyance I had has passed.

"I thought you'd never ask," she says.

I get up, and Zoey follows me out the door and down the little hill. I'm at the end of the dock before I remember I wanted a pill, but I shove the thought away. I don't even feel like having one anymore.

The water laps at the posts as I climb down into the boat, then reach up and hold a hand out.

Zoey accepts my hand, her fingers gripping mine, hot, as she steps down into the boat. "Thank you," she says.

Neither of us sits right away, her fingers still curling around mine. She's standing close, our knees almost touching, and I stare right into her eyes.

They look more blue than brown, a trick of the moonlight and the water.

The moment breaks when the boat shifts a bit, rocking enough that I have to let go of her hand and reach out to grab the dock to keep us from tipping.

"You can sit toward the front, if you want," I say, pointing to a couple of seat cushions.

"I thought maybe I'd help row," she says. "I let Liam play the gentleman earlier, but it looks kind of fun."

"Oh. Sure."

I don't even know if it'll work very well, each of us rowing one side, but I figure we can give it a shot. We sit side by side on the middle bench, facing forward so we can see where we're going, and take hold of the oars, which are secured to the side through the little rings. I untie the boat, then lean over and push us off the dock.

We drift in silence for a moment, the only sounds the water lapping against the side of the boat. The moon hangs low overhead, providing a beam of light across the lake that looks like a yellow brick road. Maybe we should follow it. Maybe it will lead us to the Emerald City, where our every wish can be granted.

"Okay, so we need to row in unison or we'll just go in circles," I say. "Ready?"

"Aye, aye, captain."

"On three. One, two … three." I dig my oar in, then push forward.

Zoey's elbow knocks into me and the boat hardly moves.

I snort as I realize she just rowed backward. "Have you ever done this before?"

"Rowed?"

I nod.

"Uh, yes?"

I smile. "You're not a very good liar."

"Okay … no?"

I pull my oar far enough in that I can rest it on my knees, then reach over to stop her disorganized movement.

I rest my hand over hers, and she stills. "It's super easy once you get going, but there's a certain way to do it that is most effective and also cuts down on splashing."

"Okay," she says.

My hand is still resting on hers. I have the urge to glance back, just to see if Liam is watching us. But we're on the opposite side of the dock, and, sitting down like this, the wood blocks both his view and ours.

"It's sort of an egg-shaped stroke. Turn the oar a bit as you put it back into the water. You want it at an angle or else you kind of slap the surface and it makes a big splash."

With one hand on hers where she grips the oar, and my other hand directly on the wood, I twist the oar until it's at the right angle, showing her what I mean as I talk.

"Okay," she says. "Like this?"

I leave my hand resting on hers as she rows forward. Just

as it's about to hit the water, I use my hand to guide her in twisting the oar juts a bit.

"Cool. I think I got it."

Reluctantly, I let go of her hand and pick up my own oar again. "Okay then. Ready?"

"Yes."

"On three. One … two … three."

We pull back on the oars, lift up to dip them back into the water, and then push forward. Again and again, until the boat is finally moving steadily across the lake, into the darkness and away from the fire. The lights from the cabin die away and the darkness soon envelops us.

We don't speak as we row, our sides and shoulders and elbows bumping periodically.

When we reach the middle of the lake, I stop. Zoey rows one more time, then pauses as well.

The one extra stroke on the left side causes the boat to turn a bit, and we sit in silence as the boat gradually drifts until we're facing back the way we came. The cabin is dimly lit, but in front of it the fire glows orange, the dancing flames reflecting on the water, glimmering.

"It's pretty," Zoey says, in a sort of breathless whisper.

"*You're* pretty," I say, without thinking.

The words are out and they just hang there, awkwardly.

"I mean, I don't know why I said that," I add hastily.

"Well, don't try to unsay it," she says in a teasing voice. "It's probably the nicest thing you've ever said to me."

I train my eyes on the fire in the distance, wondering if Zoey can see the flush in my cheeks.

"I'm glad I came here," Zoey says, a heartbeat later.

"Yeah?"

"Yeah. It makes me think I'm not stupid for believing life will be better if I can somehow get me and Carolyn out of Hilltop. There's a whole world outside that neighborhood, you know? I just need to figure out how to make it so that she doesn't have to go back to that school."

Her words fall heavily on my ears. The sad wistfulness of it, but beyond that, the honesty. It's at odds with her usually hard looks, and it brings back a memory.

"You were different before, weren't you? Freshman year? We had a class together. You were more . . . "

"Preppy?" she asks. "Cheerful?"

"Yeah."

Zoey nods. I wish I could make out her expression in the darkness.

"Why'd you let it all change you so much?"

She snorts, an ugly bitter sound. "I know you're not stupid, Olivia."

"I mean, I get that people have said some pretty shitty things about you, but—"

"But what?"

"But why'd you do it?" I blurt.

She sneers, and I want to close my eyes against the sight of it. "*Do it*? Are we in third grade? Your friend has no problem saying it—why can't you?"

"Why'd you sleep with Zach? Everyone knew he was dating Ava."

The sneer turns even harder, and though I can't see every

detail, when she looks over at me, her eyes meeting mine, there's enough fury that I half expect her to shove me out of the boat and row away.

"I didn't even know he was her boyfriend," she says. "I'd only been at Annie Wright for, like, a week, and obviously he didn't go there. I had no reason to connect him with Ava."

The water laps against the boat and I strain to hear her quiet voice.

"I really thought Annie Wright was my chance," she says. "We all had uniforms and I thought I could fit in, you know? Be one of the cool kids for once. So I heard about the party, and I wore my best clothes, and I went. God, I was so nervous. You have no idea."

"Why?"

"Because you and Ava were so cool, you know? I thought I could make a good impression."

I chew on my lip, staring down at where my paddle is making small ripples as the boat bobs along. "So what went wrong?"

"You guys weren't there at first. I was nervous, so I had a couple of drinks, and this guy starts talking to me. Like really noticing me and flirting with me, and it was the most empowering, intoxicating feeling. I'd felt like nobody ever saw me, but this guy, who was so well dressed and so cute, noticed me."

"Ava's boyfriend," I mutter.

"Yeah. If I'd known, I would've blown him off. But he was so smooth, you know? Made me feel like I was so one of a kind, so special. And so he tells me there's a ping-pong table in the garage, but then the next thing I know, we're in some random bedroom completely making out. I hardly even noticed when he took my shirt off."

"And then Ava—"

"Ava was looking for him, and she found him. With me, in my bra and jeans. And she blamed me for everything. Because, of course, her boyfriend was perfect, and I was the slut who went after him. That's all she could see."

Somewhere out on the lake, a fish jumps. The splash is all I can hear.

"You know what's truly fucked up?" she says.

"Everything?"

"All I wanted was for her, for you, for half the school to like me. The whole summer leading up to the start of school, I'd had this image in my head. I was going to be someone else inside that school. I was going to fit in and make friends, and somehow that was going to make everything better. Annie Wright was going to be my path out of the shitty life I had. I was so certain of it."

She sighs. "It's never been easy. But I thought if I could pull it off, things would get *easier*. And I did the one thing to ensure that it never would. I was stupid. I fell for a pretty smile and a few compliments."

Her words are heavy, and I'm almost certain I can hear them falling into the water around us, creating ripples. Just like that party.

"I've spent the last three years just trying to get through. I thought she'd get tired of it. She has a new boyfriend now. But she hates me so much she just keeps bringing it up—telling people about how I'm such a slut, that I sleep with everyone, saying they shouldn't let their boyfriends anywhere near me."

And I'd believed it all. I never doubted Ava's claim that Zoey had known who Zach was, that she'd gone after him even though Ava was his girlfriend.

"I'm sorry."

"Then prove it, Olivia," Zoey says. "Tell Ava she's wrong. See if she apologizes, and then show me where your loyalty is."

"She's her own person. I can't make her do anything," I mumble.

"If she won't stop running my name through the mud, but you still call her a friend, then you're not who I thought you were."

"Maybe if you'd just told her you didn't know, that he was the one pursuing—"

"Yeah, she'd totally believe me, wouldn't she?"

I want to say she's wrong. I want to argue it. I want it to be simple.

I find her hand in the darkness and squeeze it. She intertwines her fingers with mine, and we sit there in silence, watching Liam's shadow as he gets up and walks away from the campfire. Zoey leans against me, resting her temple on my shoulder.

"Everything got really screwed up," she says, her voice hardly more than a whisper. "People started writing stuff on my locker, and whispering stuff, and asking me if I was going to steal their boyfriends, too. I don't even know how

I would've handled it if there were guys at school thinking I was a sure thing. I guess I should be grateful for that."

"I remember some of that."

"I deleted my Facebook page because I kept getting all these mean messages."

"People can be bitches," I say, and she laughs softly at my horrible attempt at a joke.

"I got really depressed for a while. Like, really bad."

"You didn't—"

"No, I would never kill myself. Carolyn needs me. I knew I'd claw my way out of it somehow."

"I never even questioned it," I say. "I had no idea."

"It's not like I walk around telling everyone this stuff. No one at school cares about me. I'm the poor little scholarship student."

I squeeze her shoulder and relish the feeling of her curled into me, the weight of her head on my shoulder. It feels . . . right. Comfortable. Like I've waited my whole life to just be sitting here in the darkness with her, listening to her secrets.

I turn and kiss the top of her head. "You can trust me, you know that, right?" I say, my lips still against her hair.

"I told you the truth, didn't I?"

I turn back to the shore and rest my cheek against the top of her head.

"Yeah. You did."

ZOEY

I awake the next morning to the sounds of pots and pans banging around on the other side of the wall.

The kitchen.

Liam's arm is heavy around my waist, but we're both still fully clothed. By the time I got back last night with Olivia, he was asleep or passed out or something—his snoring didn't stop when I slid under the covers. It still took me a while to fall asleep because I kept half expecting him to wake up and want to hook up, but he was out cold.

I don't know what might happen tonight, but I'm sort of hoping it'll be the same. Before anything gets more serious…more physical, I need some time to figure out how I really feel about him.

All night, my head kept spinning and spinning and spinning as I thought about how Olivia had acted in the boat. As I thought about the way she'd wrapped her arm around me and just...listened.

I'm afraid to get up and go into the kitchen and have it be weird, but I'm more afraid to go in there and have it be like our conversation last night never happened.

I slide out of bed, the floor cold on my bare feet, feeling both nervous and strangely at peace. I leave the bedroom behind, pausing at the big mirror on the wall in the living room. I quickly smooth out my hair, tucking it behind my ear, and wiping away the smudged eye liner under my eyes.

Then I walk into the kitchen, where Olivia is pouring batter onto a flat grill. She beams when she looks up at me. "Hey. So, you can choose between Mickey with one-and-a-half ears, or a smiley face pancake that looks like a guy who got hit in the head a few too many times." She nods at the platter next to the grill.

I want to stare, because she's in a pink tank top and pajama pants, her hair in a low pony tail and her face make-up free. She looks prettier than I've ever seen her, in the tiny kitchen with a little blue apron tied around her slim waist.

"Nice." I grab one of the clean plates next to the platter, stab the crooked smiley-face-shaped pancake, and squeeze a liberal amount of syrup on top. I'm all too aware of the way she's watching me, and heat creeps up my neck. Unlike her, I don't look cute in the mornings, and my pajamas are mismatched. "I didn't know you can cook."

"Ah, yes. And clearly I've really been holding out on you," she says, gesturing to the pancake on the grill.

I laugh and go to the table at the end of the kitchen,

sitting down in one of the '70s style vinyl seats. I'm not sure how we're supposed to act, but when Olivia looks up a moment later, she gazes at me intently, searching my eyes.

It's enough acknowledgement. I nod, and she smiles back, and it has nothing to do with the lake or the pancakes. It's about us. It's about last night.

It's weird to think I ever hated her, ever thought she was just like Ava.

It brings me back to that first night at the condo, when I told her I was waiting to see the substance behind her pretty façade.

I see it now.

"So, I was thinking more about our project," she says, turning back to the grill.

"Yeah?" I take my first bite of pancake. I can tell it's just box mix, but it's delicious and warm and I want a hundred more.

"Yeah. I was thinking we should work together more. At my house again. It's due soon, so we need to finish it up."

"Oh. Yeah. That could work," I say. "I only have a couple of shifts at work this week."

Liam comes out of the bedroom then, and as soon as I glance over at him, I feel my cheeks warm. Not because he looks good—he does, with his hair kind of tousled and his pajama pants sitting low on his hips—but because I feel like he just caught me and Olivia in the midst of . . . something.

But we're just talking.

"Coffee," he mumbles, clearly oblivious to the shift in my relationship with Olivia.

Olivia points to the coffeemaker at the end of the counter. "Already got you covered."

He focuses on pouring himself a tall mug, and Olivia steps back to make a funny face at me behind his back.

I'm grinning from ear to ear when Liam turns and leans back against the counter, glancing over at me. I drop the smile, trying to act casual.

"You guys want to swim today?" he asks.

"Definitely," Olivia says.

He walks to the table, smelling of coffee, and kisses my temple. "Sleep well?"

"Yep. Like a rock."

Seemingly satisfied, he turns away and grabs a plate. "Hope you're planning to make a dozen more of these, because I'm starving."

"You got it, bro," Olivia says. "I'll make so many you can eat until you explode."

———

By noon, it's warmed up enough for us to go down to the dock in our swimwear. I've got a towel wrapped around me, and I'm feeling a little self-conscious and a lot excited to swim. I haven't actually swum in years, since our middle school PE class did a unit on it and we went to the local pool.

There's a big table at the end of the dock and I follow Olivia's lead, kicking off my flip-flops and tossing my towel onto the glass surface, which exposes me in all my pale, gangly glory. Ignoring the warmth of Liam's eyes on my skin, I stride to the end of the dock and, without hesitation, leap.

It's an ugly, half-assed cannonball, and as the water swallows me up, covers my head, I don't even care. The lake feels glorious on my skin.

I break the surface, grinning as I tread water. I never want to leave. I just want to float around and enjoy the slippery, soothing feeling.

I twist around, looking back up at the dock to see if they're coming too, but no one's there. I narrow my eyes, and I'm about to call out when the sound of heavy footsteps on wooden boards breaks the silence.

And then Liam and Olivia appear simultaneously, racing to the edge of the dock and leaping, flying, over my head, synchronized in their motions. For a moment I can picture them as kids practicing their jumps, doing it again and again and again.

I close my eyes against the splash, and then wipe the water from my face.

Olivia's head appears first, and I wait, poised, for Liam. *One ... Two ...*

But he doesn't appear.

And then something's grabbing my leg, yanking me under, and I take a quick gulp before the water swallows me again. When I sputter to the surface, I'm laughing and shaking off Liam's hands, kicking away from him.

"Jerk!" I say, grinning from ear to ear as I try to splash him back.

He swings his hand, and a great big wave of water monsoons toward me.

"HELP! Olivia!" I scream, pleading for assistance as her brother overwhelms me.

She swims closer and skims her hand across the water, cascading the droplets right at Liam's face.

"HEY!" he sputters, and for a moment he stops splashing me. I take my opportunity to swim closer, grabbing his shoulders and shoving him under before swimming as fast as I can to the ladder on the dock.

Olivia follows, and we make it to the steps in seconds. I get one foot onto the iron before someone's grabbing me. I turn to yell at Liam, but it's Olivia.

"Me first! He'll spare you!" she yanks me off the ladder and I fall backward, trying to squelch the laughter so I can close my mouth and not inhale the lake.

I sputter to the surface and see Olivia, halfway up the ladder, her hand outstretched. I accept it and she yanks me over, and then we're both scrambling out just as Liam reaches us.

I climb the last couple of rungs and then half fall, half roll across the wooden planks, landing on my back and staring up at the cloudless sky. My chest heaves; my body and hair are soaked. I'm blissfully happy and out of breath.

"You guys cheat," Liam calls out.

"You're the one who stealth-dunked me," I say. "So I had to get a little revenge."

Liam's coming up the ladder, so it's safe enough to go toward the end of the dock and dip my toes in the water without worrying about him popping up below me. I scoot down a few boards, then let my feet dangle below me.

Olivia follows suit, scooting over and leaving enough space between us for Liam.

He drops down between us, tossing his arm around my shoulders and dripping water down my back. "I'm going to get you for that, you know."

I lean back on my hand, turning to look him in the eyes.

"I'm kind of counting on that," I say. "But you'll never win."

I feel something over my hand and flick a glance down, realizing it's Olivia's fingers covering mine. I lean back a tiny bit more and meet her eyes. They're sparkling with amusement, like she's trying to convey something.

And then I recognize the mischievous look she's giving me. I blink twice, as if to say *Yes*, and then sit up again. I stare out at the water, leaning into Liam's body.

"So, about getting me back," I say, slowly turning my hand to interlace my fingers with Olivia's.

"Yeah?"

"Good luck with that."

Then we yank our arms forward, like a snapped rubber band, and shove him off the end of the dock.

OLIVIA

Monday afternoon, I wander the mall after school, unable to stop thinking about the weekend. Something between Zoey and me has changed, evolved. On Saturday night, after Liam started yawning and stretching and finally went to bed, we sat on opposite twin beds in the basement and talked until two o'clock in the morning before finally drifting off.

I slide my phone out of my pocket and glance at the text icon. Still no reply from Ava. The two of us need to have a *serious* chat, and it's not something we can do over the lunch table at school.

My hands are sore from a brutal day at gymnastics and my nose kinda hurts from when I missed on the uneven bars and slammed into the ground, but I don't really feel like going home. So instead I schlep from store to store, laden with bags, waiting for the moment the shopping high kicks in.

I'm at one of the little boutiques that has dark, angsty

stuff in the window—graffiti art and face-piercing jewelry and black T-shirts—and I turn the spinning rack to look over the earrings.

I'd never wear this stuff, but it reminds me of Zoey, and suddenly I want to buy her a gift. I want to hand her something and see her eyes light up, and I want her to know that I thought of her.

My eyes rove the rack, taking in the earrings that resemble pearls—except they're iridescent black. They're perfect.

I grab them off the shelf and check the price: twenty-eight dollars. Just right for a random, no-occasion gift. I take them to the front register but there's no cashier there.

"I'll be there in just a moment," a voice calls out.

I nod and study the items in the case in front of me.

Temporary tattoos. Except these look fancier than the sort I used to put on as a little kid. In place of the colorful cartoon characters, most of these are plain black and resemble real tattoos, with great details and shading.

"Sorry about that," the cashier says. "Just these earrings?"

I shake my head. "No, uh, I'll take two of those, too." I point to a tattoo in the corner of the case.

"Alrighty," the girl says, sliding two of the five dollar tattoos out and adding it to my total. "That'll be $41.42."

I hand her my plastic, and a moment later I'm carrying the little bag out of the shop.

I get my phone out and text Zoey, grinning the whole time.

———

That night I wait in my car outside of Burgerville, watching the green digits on the dash march toward ten thirty. I know I should be tired by now, but I'm totally tuned up instead.

Inside the restaurant, lights flick off and the place falls into darkness. A moment later, the door swings open. Zoey turns back to lock up, and then she glances my way, her lips curling into a smile.

Even though she can't see me, I find myself grinning back. When she gets closer, I climb out of the car and walk around the vehicle to open the door, gesturing grandly to the passenger seat.

"Your chariot awaits," I say, bowing.

"I had no idea you were such a cheeseball," she says.

"Maybe I've been watching Reese Witherspoon movies all evening," I reply. It's not true, but I did catch the end of *Legally Blonde* while I waited for it to be late enough to pick her up. Liam wasn't home yet—I don't know why—and I needed something to fill the silence.

I close the door behind her and then go back around to my seat. I'm beside her an instant later. My heart is doing crazy things in my chest, ping-ponging around like I took speed or something.

The car hums quietly but I don't put it in gear. Instead, I dig into my purse and produce a tiny gift bag. "Uh, so I kind of bought you something today."

"It's not my birthday or anything," she says, eyeballing the bag. "I don't turn eighteen till spring."

"I know, and it's not like I planned to get you anything, I was just at the mall and I saw this and I thought of you. So here." I thrust it as her, and the ribbon handle flies up so fast she flinches.

Zoey looks me in the eyes, questioningly, as she takes the bag and sets it on her lap. "Okay. Um, thank you."

"You're supposed to open it now," I say.

"Oh." She slowly reaches into the bag, and when she pulls her hand back out, the little card, with earrings, is pinched between her fingers.

"Oh my god, these are amazing," she says in a gasping sort of way. "But I can't accept jewelry—"

"It's just costume jewelry, nothing fancy," I say. "They reminded me of you, and you're not allowed to give them back because I already threw away the receipt. And they're not my style. So there."

When Zoey looks up at me, her eyes are shining in the yellow glow created by the streetlamps. "Wow. This might be the nicest thing anyone's done for me in a long time."

"There's something else in there," I say, reaching for the bag. I slip my hand into it and find the tattoo, then pull it out and show it to her.

"Wow, that's cool," she says, taking the tattoo and holding it up in the lamp light. It's a funky, scribbly heart, just an outline in all black like a real tattoo.

"I kind of got one too," I say, pulling my sleeve back and showing her the underside of my wrist.

She stares at it for a long moment and then looks up at me. There are so many things in her eyes, I don't know what she's going to say next.

But she doesn't say anything at all.

She leans over and kisses me, just the barest brush of her lips against my cheek. "Thank you," she says.

And then she goes to lean back again, and I don't want the space between us. I reach over, cupping the back of her neck with my hand, and turn her face to mine.

And then I don't give myself time to think about what I'm doing.

I just kiss her.

When my lips touch hers, it's like a missing puzzle piece clicking into place. It's like finding the right key for a lock. It's like every stupid metaphor I've ever heard.

It's right. It's more than right, it's perfect. The way her soft, warm lips feel as she parts them against me, the soft sigh that escapes, the way her long hair feels as my fingers tangle in the strands...it's all perfect.

A moment later she pulls away and we both turn to stare out the windshield, like we're not quite ready to look each other in the eye. My heart is erratic and thumping so hard I think she must hear it.

"So..." Zoey says.

"Yeah." And then I giggle like an idiot because I don't know what else to do. And then Zoey's laughing, too, and my car is filled with it, filled with the tension and the buzzing and the euphoria of our kiss—of the turning point, of this moment we walked to the cliff and jumped, together.

It feels like it must take five minutes for us to stop laughing and looking at each other, then laughing some more. And it doesn't even make sense, doesn't fit what just happened, and yet it's so right.

I just kissed Zoey, and it was perfect.

"Uh," I say, after our laughter finally dies down. "So, do you want to put that tattoo on?"

"Yes," she says.

I reach for her hand, my fingers curling around her bare wrist. Then I peel the plastic off the tattoo and gently press the paper to her skin.

"Don't move," I say, leaned over, so close she must feel my breath. Her hair falls forward into her eyes as she watches me.

I grab the water bottle from the cupholder and dribble some water onto my fingers, then press them onto the paper, onto her skin.

I hold her wrist like that, my fingers curled around her arm, the water running down her skin and dripping onto the center console. Her heartbeat pulses against my fingertips.

If I thought the kiss was magical, this is something else. It's an intimate moment in the near-darkness of my car, in the silence, as I lift her hand up and blow against the paper, drying the water.

Soon I peel the paper off, revealing a perfect, beautiful, heart-shaped tattoo.

I hold my arm parallel to hers, so the two tattoos are side by side.

"I love it," she says. "Thank you."

I look up at her, and when she leans over and kisses me a second time, my eyes slip shut and I lose myself to it.

ZOEY

I know I should be exhausted after my late shift at Burgerville, followed by texting until two or three a.m. with Olivia, but I'm not. I'm too amped up to see her. Everything that's been missing with Liam—that underlying reluctance I couldn't quite recognize—is there with Olivia.

I push my way into the crowded halls, forcing myself to look up, not at the floor like I always do.

I stop off at my locker to swap out my books, then toss my backpack over my shoulder and head to the locker bay where Olivia always sits in the morning.

I falter when I see her sitting next to Ava, but just as I ponder turning and walking away, Olivia looks up and a smile lights her face. I'm instantly warm from the inside out as I think of last night, of how it felt when we kissed again outside my house. I'm glad she has tinted windows. I wanted to kiss her over and over and over again, but eventually I got out of her car and floated to my front door.

I continue to walk toward her, watching as her smile melts away and is replaced by...something. Anxiety? Worry?

When Olivia glances over at Ava, her emotions clarify.

She doesn't want Ava to see us talking. But is it because of what we did last night...or who I am?

"Hey," I say, stopping in front of them. "I, uh, sent you my next few pages of our project."

"Oh," she says. "Okay. Cool. I'll look them over."

But her voice is flat and formal and I suddenly feel like an idiot standing here—like I'm overdressed or wearing a costume when everyone else isn't.

Like I don't belong here conversing with her. Conversing with the girl who was kissing me last night. The girl who put the tattoo on my wrist.

I glance down to see if she's still wearing hers, but she's got a long-sleeved sweater on. Did she wear it specifically to cover up the tattoo?

"Great," I say when I realize she's just sitting there, in silence, waiting for me. "Um, I think I did a pretty good job. It's coming together really well."

"Okay," Olivia says. "I'll read it during study hall."

She says nothing else, just sits there like she's expecting me to walk off. And suddenly, I'm angry. She's sitting here treating me like I'm no one. She's embarrassed by me. That's what this is. She doesn't want Ava to know we're even talking, let alone something more.

"Did you find the earring you lost?" I ask, remembering one of her last text messages.

Ava looks over at Olivia. "What earring did you lose?"

"The diamond studs she got from her dad for her sixteenth birthday," I say.

Ava and Olivia share a glance, but I can't read it.

"Oh, uh, yeah. It was under my bed," Olivia says. Her face is growing red and it angers me even more.

"Told you it would be there," I say.

"Because you know so much about beds, right?" Ava says, and then breaks into cackling laughter like she just told the best joke of the year.

Olivia swallows, staring down at her hands. She should be *defending* me.

My stomach drops, disappointment hollowing it out. "No, because Olivia said she sometimes sleeps in her earrings."

"And you sleep with just about anyone, so what's the difference?"

It's hard to breathe. Embarrassment, white-hot, shoots through me, mingling with my building fury. Between Olivia's coldness and Ava's ruthlessness, I can't help myself.

I march closer to Ava, forcing her to tip her head back to look up at me.

I'm done waiting for Olivia.

I can stand up for myself.

"You know what, Ava? I'm sick of you. I'm sick of you blaming me for a stupid ex-boyfriend who can't keep his hands to himself. I'm sick of your holier-than-thou attitude.

I'm sick of you constantly laughing behind everyone's backs. And I'm sick of you spreading lies about me."

I'm certain that every person in the hall has stopped, frozen completely to watch us, because my voice seems unreasonably loud over the normally raucous hallway chatter. I rake in a deep breath, resisting the urge to glance over my shoulder, because judging by the sudden silence, everyone is staring.

Ava moves like she's going to get to her feet, but I lean farther over, forcing her to lean back instead of stand up. "It's time to fucking move on, got it? If I ever, *ever* hear that you've spoken my name again, you're going to regret it. So back the fuck off and get out of my life."

I spin on my heel and stalk away, my heart hammering out of control. I shove my way through the crowd that seems to have tripled while I had my back turned, wanting to get the heck out before Ava can retaliate.

Halfway down the hall, someone grabs my arm and I spin on them, sure it's Olivia with some pathetic apology.

"Whoa, whoa, I'm not one of them," the girl says. Trina...that's her name. She sits next to me in science, and I loaned her a pencil a few days ago. "I just wanted to say..." Her voice trails off and she grins. "That. Was. Awesome."

Her smile is infectious. I find myself smiling back as she holds out her fist to bump mine, and I can finally breathe again. "You think?" I say. "I'm kind of terrified I just started World War Three."

"Well, consider me your ally, because Ava has been such a bitch to me for years. She dated my brother once and she thinks I convinced him to dump her."

"Did you?"

"Hell yeah. He could do way better than her."

I laugh, my heartbeat getting back under control as we head to our science class. "I thought I was her prime target."

"No. I mean, she left me alone for a little while, but when she found out that Cade—the guy she dated last year—asked me out, the claws came out again. She completely nailed me in the head during kickball yesterday."

"Ugh."

"Yeah. And just so you know, I never got why she blamed you for the thing with Zach. She's focused on the wrong person, you know?"

My chest tightens and I try not to look at her as we enter the classroom and make our way to our desks.

"Yeah, I know," I say.

"Zach is a total man-whore. He would have thrown himself at anyone, really."

I nod, wondering if anyone else in this school agrees with her.

"Well, I'm glad I have an ally, anyway," I say. "I'll probably need it."

"A lot of people don't like her, you know. Or care about what she says."

"You think?"

"Maybe they did once, but she's burned her share of bridges over the years—let's just put it that way."

Our teacher walks in then, so we get out our books. And as I flip to the right unit, my thoughts shift away from Ava and back to Olivia.

I'd gotten so angry at Ava, I'd almost blocked out the way Olivia just...sat there. Letting Ava mock me. I'd almost forgotten the way she kind of recoiled as I walked up, like she was worried about being seen with me.

It's not like I was going to waltz up and kiss her. I get that we're not going to be a public couple or anything. I don't even know for sure if we *are* a couple.

Maybe that's why Olivia reacted like that. Maybe she doesn't know what we're going to be either, and she thought I was going to be super forward or something, and she's just not ready for that.

I could be overthinking this.

But as our teacher starts class, it's all I can do not to replay that expression of hers, over and over and over.

I need to know who I am to her.

OLIVIA

Ava gets to my house at seven, breezing through the door like she lives here.

In a way, she does. We've been friends for so long, our houses are like second homes. She knows the code for the key box and doesn't even knock when she gets to this floor; she just walks right in.

So it's weird to realize that ever since school started this year, we've hardly made time for each other.

I narrow my eyes, staring at a swirl in the hardwood floors as the realization sets in. How have I hardly even noticed how little we've hung out?

"Hey," Ava says, walking to the fridge. I tear my eyes away from the floor and force a smile on my face. "How was gymnastics?"

I pull out a stool. "Eh, okay. I'm kinda struggling."

"Oh?" Ava sits down beside me, sliding one of the two cans she's grabbed in front of me.

"Yeah. I can't quite nail my floor routine. I mean, I did once, but I haven't managed to do it again."

"You'll get it. Consistency is the hardest thing, right? Just keep at it."

"Thanks," I say, popping the top on the can. "I'm not quite so certain."

As we sip the pop, the ticking of our grandfather clock seems louder than ever, as if announcing every second of awkward silence. As if pointing out every moment I've failed to stand up for Zoey.

"Um, so, I know my text was kinda cryptic," I say.

"It was very cloak and dagger. *Come to my house at seven. Come alone.*"

I elbow her. "It didn't say *come alone.*"

She snort-laughs. "I know. Geez, you're even more serious than usual. What's up?"

"I need you to apologize to Zoey," I blurt out.

She sets her can down and narrows her eyes. "Why would I do that? She totally humiliated me today! I looked like a freaking idiot."

"Come on, Av. You know you've been riding her for years. You've made her miserable. You need to let it go and move on."

"No. So not happening," Ava says, twisting on the stool to stare at me. "You can't be serious."

"I don't even get why it's all her fault. She didn't owe you loyalty, Zach did. Zoey had no idea he was your boyfriend."

"Are you seriously choosing her over me right now, after what she said today?"

I pick at the tab on my can, and it makes little hollow plinking noises. "It's not like that. It's about being the bigger person and realizing maybe you've been punishing her too long."

"Did you *see* everyone watching us? There's no way I'm going to turn around and apologize to her."

I tear my eyes away from my can. "Apologize to her or we're done."

She blinks and kind of recoils, her eyes wide. "What the hell, Olivia."

"I mean it," I say, conviction heavy in my tone. "If you want to stay friends, you're going to apologize to Zoey and then quit spreading rumors about her."

Ava laughs—a horrible laugh with exactly zero humor in it—and shoves her stool back. "I have no idea why the hell you've decided that Zoey is more important than our friendship, but I look forward to hearing from you when you come to your senses."

She yanks the front door open, just in time to reveal my brother approaching, his skateboard tucked under one arm. But instead of speaking to him, Ava all but shoves him aside as she leaves.

Liam stares after her for a moment, then rights himself again, slipping through the door with a total *what was that all about* look on his face.

"What's her deal?" he asks, stepping into the entry and kicking off his sneakers.

"I pissed her off," I say, sliding off the stool and grabbing her still-full soda.

"Obviously. What'd you do, slice her Amex? Chip her manicure?"

I pour Ava's soda down the drain. "No. I told her to apologize to Zoey."

"What?" he asks, suddenly intrigued. Like maybe our little tiff wasn't stupid girl stuff after all. "What'd she do to Zoey?"

"She's been on her case forever. It was just some stupid thing from freshman year, and I figured it had gone on long enough. But apparently Ava's not one for letting go." I blow out a long, drawn-out sigh.

"If it happened three years ago, why do you care about it now?"

"They kind of got into it in the hall today. I decided enough was enough."

"Huh. I'm surprised she didn't mention it."

I dart a look at my brother. "Wait. Were you with her just now?"

"Yeah. I took her over to Foss," Liam says.

"Ugh, you made her hang out at the skate park?"

He shrugs. "She seemed into it. I taught her how to do a manual and an ollie."

I narrow my eyes. "She mastered two tricks in, like, an hour?"

Liam grins. "Okay, so she didn't really complete the tricks, but there's always next time." He grabs a mini-bag of Doritos out of a nearby cupboard, walks to the living room, and sits down, his feet up on our glass coffee table.

I follow him, soda in hand. "And you expect me to believe she thought it was fun?"

Okay, it's not actually that far-fetched. I could see Zoey enjoying a few extreme sports. More than I ever would, anyway.

"Yeah. This chick's pretty awesome. She just kind of rolls with it, you know?"

"Wow, what a romantic speech. Let me call Hallmark."

Liam picks up one of the little decorative pillows and tosses it at me. "Shut up. I'm just saying…I really like her."

I blink. "*Really* like her?"

"Yeah. I mean…she's just different, you know?"

"I know," I say. God, do I ever. "But you're not, like, set-tling down or committing or whatever, are you?"

He can't. They can't get serious. Not if Zoey and I start seeing each other. That's…

That's weird. I can't date my brother's girlfriend.

"I'm not seeing anyone else, if that's what you're asking," Liam says.

"It's just…I figured you'd get bored of her soon."

"I thought you liked her," he says.

And for one terrifying moment, as his eyes search mine, I think he knows.

And then I realize the question is completely innocent.

"I do. We have a class together and we're working on that assignment. It's due in a few days, and she's doing a pretty awesome job at it. If we don't get an A, I'll be shocked."

"So then why do you care? I mean, with Shannon, I get it. She was dumb as rocks. And Dani ... was kind of high maintenance. And Lilli turned out to just be a bitch. You were right about them. But Zoey ... I think I could fall for her, you know?"

I know.

"Oh," I say, panic building. "Um, I see."

This is bad. Really bad. He can't fall for her.

"Anyway, I gotta shower. We were at the skate park for a long time."

He gets off the couch and leaves me there, all curled up under the soaring ceilings, feeling too small in the expansive space.

Liam actually wants to be with Zoey, as her boyfriend. Maybe for a long time, even.

He can't know what Zoey and I are to one another. Not until we figure out if it's something real, something that could last.

He doesn't need to know.

No one needs to know.

ZOEY

On Wednesday, much to my surprise, Olivia shows up exactly at seven. We haven't talked since the *incident*, and I figured she'd choose to forget about the dinner plans we'd made during our late-night text session.

I climb into the passenger seat, just to give her a chance to apologize, but she pulls away from the curb without a word.

By the time we hit the freeway, the silence feels heavy. The sun is dipping lower in the sky behind us, but the warmth of the fall night is enough that we can roll down our windows. The breeze kicks in, and my loose hair swirls around my shoulders.

"I talked to her yesterday," Olivia says, finally breaking the silence. "About you."

"Who?"

"Ava."

"And?"

She twists her hands around the steering wheel. "And I think I might need to find a new lunch table for a while."

I cringe. "It went that well, huh?"

She nods. "Yeah. She didn't really like what I had to say." Then she flicks a glance over at me. "But I should have said it right then, in the hall at school. I should have taken your side. I'm sorry I didn't."

I lean back against the leather seat. I want to agree—I want to push her—but I know this should be enough. She's choosing me over her best friend. She's standing up for me.

And that's plenty.

"So, I shouldn't hold my breath for an apology?" I ask.

"Um, no," Olivia says, squeezing my knee. "Definitely not."

"Are you okay?" I add. As much as I thought it was stupid, her being friends with Ava, I can't ignore that they were best friends. And she's just given her up.

For me.

Olivia nods. "I'll survive."

"You sure? She's kinda your best friend. As much as I hate her, I don't want to ruin that. For your sake, not hers."

"I'll be fine. And maybe she'll come around eventually."

"Okay," I say. "Thanks. But, uh, where are we going exactly?"

"I thought we could go to the Lodge," Olivia says, pulling into the fast lane. "It's in Seattle, right by the stadiums."

"Seattle, huh? That's kinda far."

"Forty-five minutes tops."

I stare at her, waiting for her to say more, waiting for her to explain.

"Okay, yeah, it's far. But I thought it made sense to go out of town where we wouldn't run into anyone."

"That's what I figured," I say. There's tension in the car, and it's making me feel all itchy and squirmy. I'm too far out of my comfort zone.

"It's mostly my brother," Olivia offers. "Who I don't want to run into, that is. I told him we were going to work on our paper at the library."

"Oh."

"So, did you have fun with him?" she asks, glancing over at me. "At the skate park last night?"

"Yeah. It was cool, learning to skateboard. I've never tried it before. Turns out I suck at it."

Olivia laughs. "I've never even tried it. I think I'd break my nose or something."

She doesn't say anything else, and I stare at the dashboard clock until it ticks over another minute. "Is that what you're really asking? If I had fun skateboarding?"

The only sign she's heard my question is the way her fingers tighten around the steering wheel.

"No."

"It's more about *him*, isn't it," I say. "About whether I like being with him."

"Yes."

"I did. I always do. Liam is a good guy."

"I know. He *is* my brother."

"That's not really what you're after, though, is it?"

157

She shakes her head but doesn't speak.

"Well, I want you to know that it's not the same with him," I say. "It's not like it is with us."

Olivia glances over at me, her surprise evident. "Yeah?"

I nod. "I think I should break up with him. I want to be with you, not him."

Her fingers tighten even more. She's hanging on to the wheel as if at any moment the car is going to try to drive off without her.

"You can't," she says.

I narrow my eyes. "I can't pick you?"

"You can't pick."

I sink farther into the bucket seat, propping my knees up against the glove box. "You *want* me to date both of you?"

"It's still so new. I mean, I didn't even know I wanted to kiss you until forty-eight hours ago. We should figure it out before you make any decisions. I don't want you to dump him or anything, because—"

"It's funny," I interrupt.

"What's funny?"

"I always saw you as this self-absorbed, selfish person, and here you are trying to gift me to your brother."

Olivia rubs her lips back and forth as if she just applied lipstick and is trying to even it out. "That's not what I meant. I just want to figure this out... what we have. What we are to each other. The thing is, you really mean something to me, and I've never felt that way about anyone before. And it's kind of scary and new and strange, and... let's just figure it out before you do anything about Liam."

"It's not going to change the fact that I don't feel anything real for him."

"I know. But if you dump him it just … it makes what we have too …"

"Overwhelming? Serious?"

"Yeah," she says. "It just puts pressure on us."

"Okay," I say. *Pressure.* Something Olivia seems to have too much of as it is.

"Yeah?"

"Yeah. But not just for him," I add. "For you. Because I don't want you to freak out about it."

"Good." Olivia flicks a glance over at me, her hands relaxing. "You look nice, by the way. I really like that shirt."

I glance down at my lavender button-up. It's a much lighter color than I normally wear, and it's a soft satin. I found it in the back of my mom's closet. It's big on me, almost a shirt-dress, and I've paired it with black skinny jeans and my battered old converse.

Olivia's wearing a dress with a short hemline, and with how she's sitting, her thighs are exposed. I have a strong urge to reach over and rest my hand on her knee, but it feels too forward.

Too real, and I don't think she's ready for that.

Soon we're at the restaurant, and Olivia finds a side street with metered parking. After we put a little sticker on the window, we walk around the block, so close that we're bumping shoulders. Once, our hands brush.

I want to grab her hand and intertwine her fingers with mine, but I don't want her to pull away, and I'm not even sure

I'm ready to do that in front of people, even if they *are* strangers. So I shove my hands into my jeans pockets instead.

The Lodge has huge wooden doors, which Olivia pulls open. She ushers me inside. It's a few steps down into the place, and as my eyes adjust to the dim lighting, I realize it's got a sort of sports-slash-hunting-lodge theme, with lots of natural wood and antlers, but not in a weird old way. More like an upscale ski lodge feel.

A hostess brings us to the back of the restaurant, to a U-shaped booth. We slide in at opposite sides but end up meeting in the middle.

"Your server will be right with you," the hostess says.

I flip open the menu, suddenly nervous again. I didn't really think about dinner that much when Olivia first asked, but abruptly I get the feeling that it's too much. Too formal. Too official. It doesn't even matter that we drove almost an hour, because it's still us, together, on a *date*. Or what feels like one.

I've never been on a date. At least, not before I met Olivia. And Liam. But with Liam it's always just "hanging out."

"I've been nervous all day," Olivia says, as if she can read my thoughts. Maybe she's just noticed the way I'm crossing my arms and raking in deep breaths.

"You don't get nervous," I say, but my own voice is a little squeaky and I giggle.

"I don't normally. But you ... this ... I was nervous."

"And now you're not?"

"Now I'm not." She squeezes my knee. I reach a hand under the table and rest it on top of hers.

"You know what's funny?" I ask, glancing at the menu.

"What?"

"Sometimes when I'm hanging out with you, I remember how badly I wanted to be part of what you and Ava were. I thought you guys were so amazing. You wore the best clothes. Everyone wanted to be you. Including me." I laugh a sad little laugh under my breath. "I guess I did get noticed by Ava, just not the way I'd planned."

Someone sets down a bread basket and I grab a piece, just to have something to do with my hands.

"So, thank you. For choosing me," I say after a few heartbeats of silence. "For giving up your friendship with her for me."

"Of course," she says. "I'll always choose you."

OLIVIA

It was perfect.
The whole night was perfect.

ZOEY

We're standing on the bow of the SS Salish, the wind whipping so hard it steals my breath away. My hair keeps tangling around my mouth.

Actually, I don't even know if there's an *SS* attached to the Salish. It's a ferry boat, not, like, something from *Gilligan's Island*.

Across the bay, the moon sinks into the water as if it's a tennis ball bobbing on the surface of Puget Sound. I lean against the green-painted metal railing and close my eyes, feeling the wind pummeling my skin. We're on the second-floor deck, too high up to feel the sea mist, but I can imagine it, the feel of the water on my cheeks.

It's not even that breezy on shore, but out here, halfway between Tacoma and Vashon Island, that's hard to believe. The water is so dark it's an inky black, as if I could leap from the boat and into the water and be swallowed whole. The boat would steam away and no one would know that I'm missing.

"It's fucking cold out here," Liam says as he emerges from the doors behind me, but there's laughter in his voice.

I turn away from the water, zipping my jacket the rest of the way to my chin and wishing I'd known to dress more appropriately. "I know. No wonder Carolyn wanted to stay inside."

"She's pretty happy with the pretzel," he says, jutting a thumb over his shoulder.

I can see her, now that I have my back to the bow. She's just inside the double doors, parked at one of the long leather benches, a table in front of her. But instead of reading the books Liam brought, she's got her face practically pressed to the window.

I look over at Liam, meeting his gaze head-on. "Thanks for letting her come. And for buying her the snack."

"Of course. She's important to you, which makes her important to me."

It's weird, hearing those words, and a million things run through my mind.

But the biggest of them all—in this moment where I feel simultaneously alone and protected, taken care of by Liam—is that I can't help but wonder what it would be like if I'd let more people in, all along. If I hadn't given Ava the power to dissuade me; if I'd found a way to make friends.

Would there be other people in my life who care about me…who cared about Carolyn? Is this what I've been missing out on this whole time?

"Was that the wrong thing to say?" Liam asks, studying my expression.

"What? Oh, uh, no. Just got me thinking."

"About?"

"About what it would be like to not feel so…"

"Alone?"

I whip around and stare at him.

"What? I get it too, you know," he says. "Our condo doesn't even feel like home. It just makes me restless." He leans against the railing, just a little bit at first, then farther and farther and farther… until he's half bent over backward, staring up at the stars, the inky black water rushing by below him. I want to reach out and grab him, pull him back, but I know he's not actually going to fall overboard.

"They always took all these trips, you know? It's not a new thing. But we had our *au pair* hanging around, taking care of us when we were younger. The first was from Germany, then two in a row from France." He stands upright again, though I'd bet it has more to do with needing to straighten his spine than wanting to look at me, because he doesn't quite meet my eyes. "There's always something… hollow inside when you realize your parents would rather work than spend time with you. I mean, they created us. You'd think they'd want to be in the same room once in a while."

It's weird. The wind is whistling across my ears, but I can hear a distinct melancholy, a wistfulness to his tone.

"I haven't seen my dad in years and years," I offer. "He doesn't even pay child support."

Liam nods slowly, resolutely, and then moves closer to

me. He grabs the railing on either side of my hips so that I'm pinned between him and the iron. But not in a trapped kind of way; in a comforting, close sort of way.

Briefly, I wonder what it would be like if this felt romantic.

If it was Olivia who was leaning in close.

I tip my head back so I can meet his hooded eyes.

"Olivia doesn't know this..." Liam trails off, then seems to get lost, staring into me.

"Doesn't know what?" I ask.

My words seem to wake him up, make him realize he's got me sort of caged between him and the railing. He steps away and we turn, so that we're both facing forward again.

The dock looms somewhere ahead, and the speakers blare to life, telling the passengers to return to their vehicles. We don't have a vehicle; we walked onto the boat for the six-thirty sailing, and the whole round trip is barely an hour. It was a short, completely for-scenic-purposes ride.

"I board this boat almost every night."

I narrow my eyes but I don't turn to him. The tone of Liam's voice says he's not quite comfortable with what he just revealed, that he doesn't want to meet my eyes.

"You what?"

"The last ferry leaves Point Defiance at 10:30. I'm usually on it."

"You ride the ferry every night? Alone?"

"Yes."

"Why?"

He doesn't speak for a long time, and I think the boat's going to dock and everyone's going to get off and the ferry workers are going to find us up here and kick us off, and still he won't have spoken.

But instead, with the docks looming, he breaks the silence. "Because I can't sleep. And sometimes I'm ... " he sighs. "Lonely. And somehow being on the water is soothing. The dock is less than ten minutes from my house. It's hardly an inconvenience. If I'm not going to sleep anyway, I'd rather be on this boat. Listening to the water and the fog horns, watching people go back and forth from the island."

"You have Olivia."

"I know."

"How have you kept this from her?"

He zips his hoodie all the way to his chin, hunching into it. "Sometimes I go directly to the docks from my friends' houses. Sometimes I sneak out after she's in bed, or when she's working on homework."

"You should talk to her," I say. "She doesn't like that you're pulling away. She's scared."

"It's a weird thing, you know," Liam says, just as the boat finally arrives, bouncing off the black-rubber sides of the ferry dock.

"What?"

"Pushing her to be her own person ... and still wanting her to be there when I need her."

I smile, willing myself not to tear up from his words, knowing how much Olivia needs him, too. "I think you should tell her that," I say, just as the door behind us swings open and Carolyn walks onto the foredeck.

Liam sighs, his shoulders rising and falling dramatically. "Yeah. Maybe I will."

OLIVIA

"I can't believe you even have all this crap," Zoey says, standing in the middle of a pile of junk, her hands on her hips. "How does one family accumulate all this stuff?"

I chew on my lip and survey the piles of boxes I promised my dad I'd get rid of. I don't even know why I'm doing this today—my parents probably won't show up for another few weeks.

I sigh. "It just looks like a lot when it's all stuffed into one room. We haven't touched it since we moved here."

Zoey snorts and then slaps a hand over her mouth, and I try not to laugh at the ugly sound. "Wait—you haven't always lived here?" she asks.

"Nope. Mom thought we should downsize."

"And … how is your monstrous condo a downsize?"

I click the lid back on a giant Tupperware container that, as it turns out, is filled with my mom's hand-me-down "antique" quilts. She'll have to sort through that one herself. "Have you ever seen that big purple Victorian up on Yakima street, in old town? Like a super monstrous one?"

Zoey narrows her eyes. "The one with the white shutters and a dinosaur sculpture in the middle of circular drive? With gargoyles or something near the sidewalk?"

"Yeah. The big sculpture is a horse, actually. It's just really old. But anyway, that's where I grew up."

"Holy shit," Zoey says. "That house is insane."

I giggle. "Yeah. It was beautiful. And creepy at night, but also amazing."

"Why'd you move?"

I screw my lips up to the side. "My parents were taking more and more trips. I guess they were worried about us in such a big house, or maybe they figured it was overkill. The condo's more secure and requires no maintenance."

"Ah."

I trace my finger over the red Sharpie words written on the next box, which spell out *China*. "The move was sort of the beginning of the end, as far as our family time went. Liam and I were sixteen and had our own transportation, and they knew we were safe in the condo. Heck, we don't even have to leave the complex to go out to dinner or to the movies."

"I see," she says.

"But it feels like a shelf to me."

"What?"

"I've always felt like they bought the condo because it's a kind of shelf. They can put us up on the shelf and then go do whatever they want, and whenever they breeze back into town, they'll take us off the shelf and ask us how we are, and drag us to a couple of parties or events to show what great parents they are, and then when the week is up, they can put us back on the shelf again."

"Oh."

"Sorry. That's probably enough whining for the day. In any case, the move is what led to this heaping pile of junk."

Zoey spins in a slow circle, as if taking it all in.

"Aren't you glad you showed up?" I ask.

She grins, grabbing a faded orange Nerf football from a nearby wire crate and hurling it at me.

I barely have time to react before it bounces off my shoulder. "HEY! So uncalled for."

"Oh come on, you owe me at least that much," Zoey says. "I was lured here under false pretenses."

"I said I needed your help!"

She flashes me an *oh please* look. "I figured it was *Olivia* style help. Like picking out the right shoes to match your outfit. And, by the way, wrong choice."

I gasp, picking up the football and tossing it back at her. "Not nice!"

Zoey catches it, grinning from ear to ear. "I'm only kidding. You actually look pretty great. But seriously, if I had known I'd be sorting through approximately one thousand pounds of stuff, maybe I would've pretended to be busy."

"Gee, thanks," I say, grinning. I can't really blame her. This place is crammed.

I open one of the boxes near her, revealing a pile of Legos. "I forgot all about these. Liam was obsessed forever. His whole room was covered in Lego creations and he refused to disassemble anything."

"Really? What did he like building?"

"Totally nerdy stuff. He had this serious *Star Wars* thing forever. His whole room was decked out. The Legos were mostly spaceships or whatever."

She giggles. "And here I thought he was super alternative," she says, making air quotes.

"Please. He couldn't *buy* street cred. The whole skater dude thing only happened in the last couple of years. Even now he's like half jock, half skater. I guess he's still figuring it out."

I open another box, pulling out a frilly, white, lace-trimmed dress. It's weird seeing all this stuff. It makes me want to dig into one after another after another and get lost in the memories.

I want to share them all with Zoey.

"And how about you?"

"I've always been . . . this," I say, holding the dress up. I tuck the hanger under my chin and drape the dress against my chest. "Girly girl. My mom modeled a little when she was a teen. I always thought her pictures were the epitome of glam. She didn't want me to get into it, though. Not officially. So she'd let me dress up and wear makeup and we'd take a bunch of snapshots and then print them out and staple them together like they were little portfolios."

Zoey grins. "Your mom sounds cool."

"She is. Was. I don't know anymore. I mean, we used to be close. She'd pretend to be a designer who was auditioning models, and I'd dress up and use my fake portfolio and do my runway walk, and she'd be like *fabulous, darling!*" I say, throwing my arm up into the air like my mom does when she gets animated.

Zoey's smile melts away and she studies me with an intensity that's just this side of disconcerting. "Do you miss her?"

I shrug. "Liam and I spent a month in Europe with them over the summer. By the end I was happy to have my space again. But sometimes, yeah."

Narrowing her eyes, Zoey sticks her thumb out to the side, as if she's concentrating, and makes a fake picture frame with her fingers and thumbs as if she's trying to imagine a camera shot.

I roll my eyes and throw the dress at her. It clobbers her over the head.

"Hey!"

I reach into the box and find another dress, this one pink, and throw it at her just as she's peeling the first one off her head.

And then I throw another and another, until the box is empty and she looks like a coatrack. The stack of dresses trembles as she laughs. "This is what I get for helping!" she says, but her voice is muffled underneath all the layers.

I laugh, too, walking closer and pulling the top dress off the pile. The others kind of drag away with it and drop to the ground. Her hair is all raked forward, almost entirely covering her face.

I reach out, pushing her hair back and tucking it behind her ear.

Zoey stills, meeting my eyes.

I don't know who moves first, or if we're pulled together by force—this undeniable attraction we have for each other—but soon my mouth meets hers and I close my eyes, enjoying the taste of her on my lips.

It's right. When we kiss, it's always right.

Something creaks beside me, and I realize a heartbeat later that it's the door to the storage room. I leap back so fast my heels hit a box behind me and then I fall, crashing into a pile of boxes that were stacked waist-high.

I land in a heap, the other stuff falling around me, until only my arms and head are left uncovered.

"Nice one, sis," Liam says as the dust settles. "Very graceful."

I can see by his flippant, amused grin that he didn't see Zoey and me.

Whew.

I swallow. "Thanks," I say, struggling to get back to my feet. I feel like I fell butt-first into a hole. "So, are you just going to just stand there, or…?"

He steps forward and extends his hand, pulling me easily to my feet.

I lean over, wondering how it is he hasn't noticed or acknowledged Zoey, but all I see is the door, swung wide enough that it's just shy of hitting the wall.

Oh. She's behind the door.

She's hiding.

From her own boyfriend. Because she's here, with me, and we didn't tell him that part.

"Did you need something?" I ask, dusting off the seat of my pants.

"Nah. Saw your text about cleaning out the storage unit and I thought I'd see if you needed any help."

"Seriously?" I ask before I can stop myself. Why the hell is he volunteering for manual labor?

"Yeah. You shouldn't have to do it yourself. Plus, you know, we haven't hung out much lately."

"Oh." I flick a glance at the door. Zoey's leaning over just enough that I can see her eyes, and she slowly shakes her head, confirming what I already know—she doesn't want to be seen. "Um, no thanks," I say. "Actually, I was going to listen to my iPod." I tap my back pocket. Even though it's not actually there.

"Dude, for real? You're going to clean this whole place yourself?"

I nod, my eyes wide and hopefully sincere. "Yep. I could use the exercise."

Liam chokes back laughter. "All right then. Suit yourself."

"Yep. I will."

I will suit myself? What does that even mean?

I stand in the middle of the room as he walks away, pausing to reach over and grab the doorknob. He glances at me over his shoulder as clicks the door shut behind him.

Revealing Zoey.

"Holy shit, that was close," she says.

"Why'd you hide behind the door?" I whisper. "I could have played it off! We're allowed to be friends. But then you're all cowering behind a door, and if you popped up five minutes later, *that* looks suspicious."

"I don't know! It kind of swung over and covered me up, and I just went with it!"

We dissolve into giggles, and I flop down on top of one of the collapsed boxes. "If you hadn't hidden, we could've had help."

"And now we're stuck in here all by ourselves. For… hours…" she says, her voice trailing off mischievously as she grabs a box, slides it up next to me, and plops down.

I turn my head to meet her eyes and our noses almost brush.

And then we kiss, and I think perhaps this room will get cleaned out another day.

ZOEY

"So ... why are we here again?" I ask as I plop down on the old wooden park bench.

"It's a surprise," Olivia says, twisting around to face me, pulling one knee up on the bench.

We're in the middle of Wright Park on a Sunday morning and I'm not sure why.

"If I'd known we were coming here I would have invited Carolyn," I say. "I'm pretty sure she'd live here if she could."

"We're not staying." Olivia digs into her enormous hand-bag and pulls out a *Cosmo* magazine.

"Uh, we came here to read magazines? Because, you know, I didn't bring one."

"No. I just needed someplace to sit for a minute, and my brother is home so I didn't want to go there."

"Okaaaaaay," I say, reaching over to rip a leaf off a nearby rhododendron. "So are you going to read me some makeup tips or something? Because, you know, that's not really my idea of a good time."

"No, silly. I have this for the quiz on page forty."

I scrunch up my nose. "People actually do those things? I always thought they were stupid."

"Shush," Olivia says, pulling a pen out of her bag. "You're just going to have to go along with this."

"Um, okay."

"Good. Favorite Restaurant?"

"Uhhh ... Olive Garden." I rip the rhododendron leaf in half, letting the pieces flutter to the ground.

She kind of snarls her lip. "If you could go *anywhere*, you'd seriously pick the freaking Olive Garden?"

"What?" I ask, surprised by her reaction. "I like the breadsticks."

"You're really lame."

"Well, if we're really talking *anywhere*, I actually like Jimmy Macs more. Does that make you feel better?"

"What's Jimmy Macs?"

"A barbecue place in Federal Way. You can throw peanut shells on the ground. I've only been there once, but it was fun."

"Okay then, I'm putting that one down. It sounds better than Olive Garden."

I laugh and reach out, pinching her knee. Olivia leans away, half-closing the magazine. "No peeking."

"Wasn't trying to."

She sits up and clears her throat. "Okay. Now, describe your dream outfit."

I try not to laugh. "Um, nice jeans and a funny T-shirt, I guess. Definitely not a skirt. I get my fill at Annie Wright."

"Of course. And what about shoes or accessories?"

"Oh. Um, Converse. I want a pair of those Dr. Seuss ones. And some kind of chunky jewelry, I guess."

"All right. Next question: favorite local attraction?"

I stare at the ground for a long moment, trying to decide. "The Pantages?"

She looks up from her magazine, her surprise evident. "You mean the theater?"

"Yeah."

"You've been in there?"

I laugh. "What, I don't look like the theater type? We went to that play freshman year, remember? During school hours? I really liked the building. It's cool, with all the little balconies and carved woodwork and stuff."

"Oh, yeah." She scribbles it down, her pen scratching across the page. "Okay, if you could do one thing you've never done before, what would it be?"

"Graffiti," I reply. "What kind of quiz is this? I thought they were always multiple choice."

She ignores my question. "Of all things, graffiti? Seriously? I thought you'd say sky-diving or swimming with sharks or something more exotic."

I shrug. "I walk by the Garage sometimes and it always looks fun."

"Is that the parking garage place where everyone paints? Down on Broadway?"

"Yeah."

"Huh. Okay." Olivia scribbles it down, but as she's writing, the magazine slips a little, revealing a lined sheet of paper.

"You're not even writing in the magazine, are you? I knew this was a weird quiz."

I reach for the magazine but she yanks it away. "That's okay. I'm done," she says, stuffing the *Cosmo* back into her bag and holding up the paper, revealing my list of answers in her perfect, swirly writing.

"What's that?" Even though I know my own answers, I still reach out and grab it, my eyes glancing over the sheet as if it'll explain what she's up to.

"Our itinerary."

"Huh?"

"First we're going to the mall, and you're going to get your dream outfit. Then we'll go to Jimmy Macs for lunch, followed by...something at the Pantages. I don't even know if they have any shows or whatever today. But after that, it's graffiti time."

My jaw drops. "You tricked me into telling you what I wanted to do? Why?"

Olivia beams. "Because if I was all *hey, let's do everything you want to do*, you'd be lame and pick things you thought I'd want to do. And you wouldn't let me buy you any clothes."

I narrow my eyes. "You don't need to buy—"

"HEY! You're going along with this plan whether you like it or not," Olivia says.

"Why?"

"Because you're always worried about everyone else and

not yourself. Today is about you. Accept this or I'll punch you in the nose." She stands up.

I smirk. "I'm rubbing off on you."

She mutters something under her breath, then extends her hand. "Come on, the mall should be open by now."

It takes me a minute to move, because I'm can't stop staring at her with a mixture of surprise and awe.

No one's ever done something this nice for me. Ever.

"Okay. Fine. Let's do it."

"Great. Your dream day starts now."

OLIVIA

I shove open the double doors of the Pantages theater, blinking against the bright sunlight.

"That was amazing," Zoey says, breathless. "I can't even believe how graceful those women are. Or how flexible."

"I'm surprised you were so into it," I say, leading her down the sidewalk.

"Why, do I not look like the ballet type?" she says, motioning to her body with a wide grin. She's wearing a pair of snug, deep blue jeans, a belt made from an old seat belt, and a bright yellow T-shirt sporting a green dinosaur with a speech bubble that says *all my friends are dead.* Her requisite "chunky jewelry" consists of a blue bracelet with giant blocky beads.

We couldn't find the Dr. Seuss Chuck Taylors she was after, so she settled for a pair of tan camo ones. And now I know what I can get her for Christmas or her birthday or something.

I blink, realizing how far ahead I'm looking. Christmas is almost three months away. Her birthday's not even until April.

The outfit seemed to have transformed her the moment she put it on, because she's been smiling and laughing and embracing everything we've done so far, even if we were both a little underdressed for ballet at the Pantages. I always feel like I'm going back in time when I set foot in there—like I should be wearing some fancy old ball gown, and that when I leave I'm going to climb into a carriage, not a car.

We walk down the hill, side by side, toward where my car sits on Broadway Street. I pop the trunk and pull out a Home Depot plastic bag. The paint cans we bought clang together as I slam the drunk shut.

"I can't believe we're going to do this," I say. "It seems like such a random thing."

Zoey grins, grabbing the bag out of my hands. "I had no idea spray paint was so cheap. I probably would've done this sooner."

"I call the pink," I say.

"What exactly are you going to paint?"

"I have no idea."

"And yet you know it will be pink."

We walk the blocks between the Pantages and the Garage in just a few minutes, and soon I'm standing at the open side of the space, staring inward.

"Wow," I say, walking to the first wall, where an enormous,

rainbow-colored face stares back at me. It looks Tribal or Aztec or something, with a huge headpiece and piercing dark eyes. "I had no idea this stuff would be so beautiful."

"Look at this one," Zoey says, pointing to the next section of the garage where a huge lion's head, mouth open wide in an eternal roar, has been painted.

We wander farther into the space, taking in the urban art. "These people have serious talent," I say.

"It's don't think I want to cover any of this up," she says, spinning in a small circle. "We could do something on those posts, though."

I turn to see where she's pointing. There are four square posts in the center of the garage, about eighteen inches across on each side. "Yeah, let's do that. I don't want to paint over something with my kindergarten-level art. And those posts look like they haven't been painted in a while."

We cross the garage and Zoey dumps out the cans, lining them up in a row between the two center posts. Pink, purple, red, green, blue, yellow, black, and a metallic gold.

She picks the black can and walks around the post, so that I can't see her. The *shhhhhhhhh* sound of the can disrupts the silence.

"What are you going to do?" I ask, grabbing the pink can.

"Not telling you," she says. "Paint on the other side of the next post and when we're both done, we'll reveal it."

"I feel like you've watched one too many HGTV shows," I say, rounding the pillar.

I stare at my pillar for a while, trying to decide what to create, before settling on an idea.

It takes us both twenty minutes of near silence, the only sounds the hissing paint or the rattling bead whenever we shake the cans. Every time I glance over at Zoey, she's got her eyes narrowed in concentration.

"You look cute when you do that," I say, snapping the lid back on my can.

"Do what?"

"Chew on your lip when you're really concentrating."

"Oh." She smiles, her cheeks flushing. "Thanks."

She sweeps her can back and forth a few more times, putting the finishing touches on her art. "Okay, so I think I'm done. You can't laugh, though."

"Hey, fine with me. But that goes both ways."

"Deal. I want to see yours first."

Zoey walks past me, rounding the pillar. She stops in front of my painting, her arms crossed, her eyes sweeping over my so-called art. "Wow. This is really pretty."

I step up beside her, studying my creation. Two sunflowers, their stalks intertwined, reach up toward a pink sunshine. One yellow petal flutters to the ground.

"Thanks. I couldn't get the leaves quite right," I say, pointing to the funky little leaves on the stalks.

"It's beautiful, though," she says.

"I don't hate it," I say, grinning. "Now let's see yours."

I walk around the pillar, stopping when I catch a view of her piece.

The center is two hearts, overlapping, one red, one black. She copied the outline of the hearts over and over, the colors alternating, until paint covered the whole pillar.

"Wow," I say. "It's amazing."

"You think?" she asks.

"Yes. It's us, isn't it?" I turn to meet her eyes.

She nods.

"I love it."

"Thank you," Zoey says, her voice serious as she runs her hands through her hair. "And not just for the compliments, but for all of today. For this." She motions to her clothes. "And for lunch, and the ballet, and the painting."

I grin. "I've had fun."

"No one's ever done anything this thoughtful for me before," she says.

"Well, get used to it."

"I'm trying. It just takes some adjustment."

"I'm not going anywhere, so you've got time."

The words are out of my mouth before I realize it, and Zoey's expression shifts.

"We're really doing this, aren't we?" she asks.

"Doing what?" I say, playing dumb.

"Being together. It works. You know it does."

I nod.

"So, I have to break up with Liam soon."

I rake in a ragged breath. "I know. Just...just not yet."

"Liv—"

"It's only been a week," I say. "It could still fall apar—"

"That's not what you're worried about," Zoey says, bending down to gather up the spray paint. "You're worried that he's going to be mad at you."

She's right.

"I pretty much stole the only girl he's ever been truly into," I mumble.

She stands up and the paint cans clang together, more hollow-sounding than before. "Even without you in the picture, I knew I didn't feel the right things for him. Breaking up with him is as much about me and him as it is about me and *you.*"

I grab the last can of paint and drop it into the bag. "I know. I just have to figure out how to do this without him freaking out, okay? Just give me a few more days. A week, tops. It needs to come from me."

Zoey steps forward and wraps me in a hug. "Deal."

ZOEY

After my short shift at Burgerville, I hurry home, half jogging, half walking to cover the mile as quickly as possible. My mom has a job interview and had to leave Carolyn at home. My sister is too young to be home by herself for long, especially in our neighborhood.

I walk the same way Olivia drove me just a couple of weeks ago, but today the sky is a vibrant blue, broken up only by a few high, fluffy clouds. Soon I'm crossing our lawn, climbing the steps, and pushing through the open door.

Inside, Carolyn is sitting on the couch, her feet propped up on the battered coffee table. Her eyes light up as I enter the living room. I grin and swing my backpack off, digging out a crispy chicken sandwich—no mayo or lettuce, her favorite— and tossing it at her.

"Oh man, I am so starving," she says. "Thanks."

I nod. "How long has Mom been gone?"

"Half hour or so."

I glance at the calendar, which has a date circled in red. My mom doesn't get many interviews, and this one made her especially nervous because it's for a supervisory position. She's never been a boss before.

"No one called or knocked on the door?" I ask.

Carolyn shakes her head. "Nope," she says, glancing up at the clock and then swallowing. "It's only just down the road, you know. She should be home any time."

"Yeah." I glance around the house, at the old newspapers piled up, at the empty glasses perched on side tables, at the dust swirling in the air. "Maybe we should clean up or something. So that if it goes like the last one … "

Carolyn takes another big bite. "Do we have to?" she says, around the food in her mouth.

"Yeah. Come on," I say. As frustrated as I get with my mom's inability to move us out of Hilltop, I know she's really doing everything she can to give us a better life. "You know how down she gets when interviews don't go well. Let's just do something nice for once."

"Fine," Carolyn grumbles.

"I'll put my stuff away."

I head to the room I share with my sister and toss my backpack down onto my unmade bed. I change out of my Burgerville polo shirt and into an old, faded Seahawks T-shirt, then return to the living room. Carolyn is balling up her sandwich wrapper and heading to the kitchen to toss it.

I go to the old boom box on the side table and flick it on to KISS 106.1, and a Katy Perry song blares through the speakers. Then I head to the kitchen and start unloading the dishes. I hand Carolyn the basket of silverware and then grab some glasses. "How's school?" I ask, putting things in the cupboard.

"It's okay. I have to make a pyramid by Monday," she says. "It's our first big assignment of the year."

"Out of what?" I ask, pushing the top rack of the dishwasher back in.

"Whatever I want." She puts the silverware basket back in the dishwasher and grabs the plates I hand to her.

"Do you want help?"

"Yeah. Talia turned hers in early, and it's really cool. She made it out of Jolly Ranchers."

"In that case, we're building the pyramid to end all pyramids. You will totally *own* this assignment."

Carolyn laughs. "I'm in."

"I'll take out the garbage. But you get to vacuum."

"Sounds like a deal." Carolyn brushes past me and heads to the living room, dancing and humming along to the radio.

I grab the garbage and head out to the backyard, to where our big cans are, enjoying the warmth of the sunshine and feeling strangely happy, in control. It helps that it's Friday, I guess.

I hear my mom's car, the familiar rumbling of the broken exhaust. Rounding the side of the house, I watch as she pulls to a stop, my heart climbing into my throat. I want this to have gone well. She's desperate for that one chance.

I shield my eyes from the sun as the car door flings open and my mom gets out. At first I can't see her expression because she turns back to the car and grabs a couple of small grocery bags.

But when she stands up, turning toward the house, she catches sight of me. And she beams, a mega-watt smile that sends hope whooshing through my veins.

I walk toward her and she meets me near the front corner of the house, where she drops the bags and flings her arms around me.

"I got it! I got it I got it I got it." She hugs me and jumps up and down. We end up kind of dancing and spinning in circles, right there in front of the house. I should be embarrassed, but I can't muster humiliation when all I feel is hope. It's like a set of wings has just unfurled and is about to take us far, far away from this dump.

"Really?" I say, even though I know she wouldn't lie. "They offered it to you right there, on the spot?"

"Yes. Five dollars more an hour, plus a full forty hours a week. *And* benefits."

"Oh Mom," I say, blinking back the tears. "That's great."

"I want you to cut back on your hours at Burgerville," she says, her words coming out in a rush. "And I want to get us an apartment in a better area. And we can get cable again, and—"

"One step at a time," I say, laughing. "I'll keep my hours the same for a little while and we can get caught up on bills. Maybe in a month or two I'll cut back."

And just like that, the long, black tunnel has a light at the end, a shining beacon, and I feel a little less lost.

Mom glances over at me, her face melting into what I can

only describe as a tender smile. "Oh, Zoey. You've grown up so much lately."

I smile, hugging her again. "Let's just go inside and tell Carolyn the good news, okay?"

I pick up my mom's dropped bags and follow her into the house, to where Carolyn is just plugging in the vacuum. She glances between us and I nod, and then she's dropping the cord and practically leaping at Mom, hugging her.

It must take a full twenty minutes before we're done hugging and laughing, and we collapse onto the couch in a heap.

It's the most surreal moment—the autumn sun slanting through the window, the three of us basking in the glow of the good news.

And, in this moment, I think I might actually be okay.

OLIVIA

My back tuck is off the moment I leave the ground. I know it. I tuck my head and pull my knees up tight, but I don't have the right momentum and I'm going to hit the floor at the wrong angle.

I land on my toes and my body keeps spinning, and then I tumble onto my back, roll over, and land on my stomach. "Ooof," I say, resting my forehead on the floor. I close my eyes, bracing for the wave of pain and the yelling. Always, the yelling.

"Olivia! What do you call that, exactly?"

I lift my head off the floor and glance over at Coach Vicks.

Right on time.

I rake in a breath, glad, at least, that I didn't get the wind knocked out of me for the second time today. "Failing spectacularly?" I ask, climbing to my knees and rocking back to sit on my heels. I look down and dust off my leotard.

"That wasn't even close," she says, striding over to where I'm sitting. "You've looked like crap lately. You used to be on top, and now . . . "

Her voice trails off. She doesn't have to finish the sentence; I can do it myself.

To avoid meeting her gaze, I look down at my hands, dusting off what remains of the chalk I used earlier for the bars.

"I don't . . . " I breathe deeply. "I don't know."

"You look weak," Coach snaps. "And uncoordinated."

"I *feel* weak and uncoordinated," I snap back. I don't need her pointing out the obvious. Every day is torture. Every day I push harder and harder, sweat more and more, and I just get worse.

"Maybe you should be putting in more time," she says. "You need to really commit if you expect to improve at this level. You're only doing two hours a day. It's no wonder—"

"Maybe I should be putting in less time," I reply, cutting her off before I can stop myself. "It's a Saturday and I'm here *again*, trying to figure out what's not working."

And yet, as the words leave my mouth, a huge weight lifts and something clarifies. I know what's not working.

I don't love this anymore.

The triumph of mastering a new skill no longer outweighs the pain and the work and the blood, sweat, and tears.

The awards no longer satisfy me. The triumph I do feel, when I finally get something down, fades faster and faster each time. All I ever want is more, more, more, and it's created a hunger that will never be sated.

I'm killing myself in pursuit of a dream that no longer makes sense.

I look up at my coach, and her expression changes from annoyance to surprise. "It's just an off day," she says, backtracking.

"All I've had lately are off days." I stand. "And I don't think I want to do this anymore."

"You're still one of the best on the team," she points out. "We need you."

"I used to be *the* best. You said it yourself," I say. "But the fire is gone. I don't want this anymore. You've got plenty of new blood to take my place. Focus on them instead."

Coach Vicks presses her lips into a thin line and stares into my eyes, as if searching for the truth. The truth I've hardly recognized but that I know, to my very core, is right.

"This isn't who I am anymore," I say, pointing to the beam and the floor and the bars and the vault. "Gymnastics is about perfection. And I don't have the desire to find it."

And it's not just with gymnastics.

It's everything. I don't want to be perfect anymore, I want to be me. I want to be *happy*. I want the weight lifted and the stress gone, and I want to do things I actually *enjoy*.

Coach heaves a big sigh, crossing her arms. "You're sure about this?"

"Absolutely," I say. "It's probably the first thing I've done right in a long time."

"Okay," she says, staring up at the ceiling as if she can't

stand to look at me. Can't stand to see whatever talent I have being wasted.

But what would be a waste is spending one more day doing this.

One more day trying to become a person I'm never going to be.

"But if you change your mind..."

"I won't," I reply. And I know it's true. Because as I walk away—as I leave the floor and the bars and the beam and the vault behind me and the gym door slams shut—all I feel is freedom. Freedom from the pressure and the unrelenting burden I'd put on myself to be better than everyone else, better than the old me.

I stop outside the doors, fishing into my backpack for my purple pill box.

I'm done with this. I'm done freaking out over every little thing, I'm done pushing myself to be perfect at all costs. I toss the box into the garbage and then walk to my car, climb inside, and head straight to Burgerville as if guided by a homing beacon.

It's Zoey who should know this first.

I pull into the lot a few minutes later, and lock my car before heading into the restaurant.

Zoey's at the register helping an elderly man who's having trouble hearing her. She repeats "$5.82" at least three times before he understands, and then waits patiently as he counts out the eighty-two cents.

When she dumps the coins into the register and looks up, her eyes meet mine. She grins, and I find myself smiling back. There's warmth there—I didn't realize it was what I was waiting to see.

It's what I *needed* to see.

The man shuffles off, his receipt in hand, and I waltz up to the register.

"Double cheeseburger," I say. "And French fries."

She raises a brow and doesn't punch the key on the register, as if she doesn't believe I'm really ordering this.

"I quit gymnastics," I say, a heartbeat later.

One corner of her mouth lifts and she hits the key to ring in my food.

"And one of those little ice cream flurry things."

"M&M or Oreo?"

"Both."

She keys it in, then waits, as if I'm going to order more.

"It was Xanax," I blurt out, and heat rushes to my cheeks as I glance around, thankful no one is within earshot. I probably should have thought this through a little better, but the truth has been bubbling up since the moment I walked out of the gym, just waiting to be set free.

"What?"

"What I was hiding in my hand that first day we talked, in the bathroom at school. It was a pillbox. Xanax."

Zoey swallows. "Oh."

"I've been getting so stressed out all the time, and it's all I can do to hold it together. My mom had the pills prescribed a couple of years ago, but I didn't use to use them much. Lately, though, I've wanted them, more and more."

"And now?"

"I threw them away. Which was really stupid," I say, my cheeks burning. "I think I'm going to get withdrawals or something. So if I have a total meltdown in about two hours, I might have to go back to the gym and dig through the trash can."

Zoey grins and punches another key. "That'll be $6.42."

I hand her a twenty. "Do you have time to sit with me?"

She glances at the clock beside the counter. "Uh, yeah. Sure. Let me tell Rita I'm going on break."

I accept my change and go find a seat next to the window, where the sun is bathing a table in warm yellow light. A few minutes later Zoey shows up, food tray in hand. When she sets it down I realize she's doubled the order, one meal for me and one for herself.

"So, tell me about this big epiphany," she says, unwrapping her burger.

"I don't know. It's just... I can't do it anymore. I just want room to *breathe*."

She nods, her mouth full of burger.

"There was a time I really did enjoy gymnastics. In the beginning I improved really fast. I was the best, easily. And I like to be the best."

"You don't say," she jokes.

"I know, but gymnastics kind of embodied my personality. It was all about precision and drive and practice. I could be exactly the person I wanted to be every time I was out there."

Zoey studies my face. "When did it become something else?"

I take a big bite of my burger, as a way to give myself

some time to think, then chew slowly. "I guess...when it stopped coming easy. When I had to actually work for it. When I had to see what it was like to fail. And then I started hating it."

"Well, that's good," she says, tossing a fry at me.

"I wish I'd realized it sooner. But at least I finally did."

I smile. There's something about this moment, about being honest with Zoey, honest with myself, that feels freeing. Like I could float right out of here on a cloud of bliss.

"What does Liam have to say about this?" she asks, popping another fry in her mouth.

"I haven't told him yet."

"Who have you told?"

"You," I say.

"Oh." She grins.

"I just thought you'd get it," I say. "I'll tell my brother later."

"I do," she says. "Get it, I mean. I get what this means to you."

"Thanks." I crumple up the empty burger wrapper, realizing I practically inhaled the thing, and then pick up the spoon for my ice cream.

"You should try dipping your fries in the ice cream," Zoey says, doing just that. I watch in fascination as she sticks a fry right into the ice cream, scoops some up, and then pops it in her mouth.

"That's gross," I say.

"Don't knock it til you try it."

So I do as she directs, dipping the fry into the ice cream and eating it. "Huh," I say, trying another. "Pretty good."

"Yeah." She picks up a spoon and rips open the plastic wrapper. "So my mom got a new job. We should be able to move to a better neighborhood."

"That's amazing!" I say. "You must be pumped."

She nods, her smile surprisingly serious. "I am. It's weird—all of a sudden all these possibilities are there. I might actually apply to college."

We fall silent for a moment, our mouths full. Zoey sticks her spoon back into her ice cream, leveling a look at me that makes my heart skip a beat. It's…intense. Searching.

"It's been a week," she says.

"Since?"

"Since you said you'd tell your brother. Remember? You said you needed a week. You've had it."

"Tomorrow makes a week."

She stares. "So you're going to talk to him tomorrow?"

I swallow. Is that what I've just agreed to? But I can't. I don't want to. He's going to freak out. I can't just be like, *Oh hi, Liam, I'm dating your girlfriend so you're going to have to break up with her.*

"I'll try."

"You can't just try," Zoey says. "You have to."

"I know." I sit back in my chair and set down my spoon. "What time are you off?"

"Ten," she replies.

"I'll come back and give you a ride."

"You don't have to do that."

"I want to."

"Okay. Thanks."

We sit in the sun for what feels like only moments longer before Zoey's break is over and she has to go back to work.

"Uh, so, I'll see you in a bit," I say.

"Okay, see ya then," she calls over her shoulder, disappearing behind an *employees only* sign.

ZOEY

The next day, as I'm walking home from work and wondering whether Olivia has had the talk yet with Liam, I hear a deep rumble building behind me. When it slows down, I glance over my shoulder to see Liam's glossy red Jeep Wrangler.

He rolls down his window—manual, not automatic like his sister's car—and waves at me, flashing that same dopey smile I've come to know.

There's no way Olivia has talked to him yet. Not when he's flashing me that kind of a smile.

"Need a ride?"

I adjust my backpack, swinging it more fully over my shoulder as I smile back. "Sure. Thanks."

I round the Jeep and toss my bag into the backseat, then grab the roll bar and haul myself up into the passenger seat. *Six inch lift*, Liam told me the first day I rode in it. I feel like it should have been installed with a step stool attached.

It's fitting, really, that Liam would drive around in this sporty, lifted jeep while Olivia prefers something sleek and fast and pricey.

"How was work?"

Why are we talking about work? Why don't we just talk about the weather while we're at it?

Olivia really should have told him about us by now. What the heck is she waiting for?

"Zoey?"

"Uh, what?" I ask, realizing that the Jeep is moving and I'm not buckled up. I snap it into place just as Liam pulls up to a stop sign.

"I said, how was work?"

"Oh, you know, same old same old. It was pretty quiet."

"That's good."

"Mhmmm," I say noncommittally.

The Jeep roars off again, down a side street alongside Wright Park. It's quiet now, though. Dark. I absently wonder if Carolyn convinced Mom to take her here today, before the sunset and the evening chill.

"So, I was thinking," Liam says, as he takes a corner at thirty and I'm forced to grab onto the little bar in the dash.

"Yeah?"

"Yeah. Uh, so Homecoming is coming up at Stadium."

"Oh?" I ask, feigning dumb, panic rising. He can't ask me to Homecoming. I'm supposed to be breaking up with him!

"Uh-huh. In two weeks. I was hoping you'd like to go with me."

"Oh," I say, trying not to cringe. I'm not going to be with him in two weeks.

But how can I say that now? Olivia wants to talk to him first. I don't want to drive those two apart. He means too much to her.

But…I don't want to do this anymore, either. I don't want to be with Liam.

"Um, I'll have to check and see if I work that day," I say when I realize he's still staring, waiting for an answer.

"Yeah, cool. Let me know."

And then we're pulling up at my house and Liam's putting the Jeep into neutral, pulling the parking brake. I glance up at the windows, finding them blazing with light. Carolyn and Mom are definitely home.

"Oh, uh, you don't have to walk me up. My mom will want to grill you. But, uh, thanks for the surprise ride."

"Sure. Text me later, okay?"

"Yeah. Will do."

But maybe I won't have to. Maybe Olivia will talk to him first.

I realize too late he's leaning over to kiss me, but I'm half out of his Jeep and dropping to the sidewalk. I give him an apologetic smile, then slam the door and head toward my house. My phone chirps.

I smile when I see there's a text from Olivia.

Be ready in ten minutes. I'm picking you up. We only need a half hour, and then I'll bring you back home before you turn into a pumpkin.

I laugh, shoving the phone back into my pocket and

pushing my way into the house. Maybe she wants to strategize about what to say to Liam. Or, heck, maybe she wants us to talk to him together.

As I step closer inside the house, I hear it:

Music.

The beat-up boom box in the kitchen is blaring out a country song. And then I glimpse my mom, boot-scootin' sideways across the cracked, stained vinyl, followed quickly by my sister.

"Heel, toe, heel, toe, twist," my mom calls out over the music, apparently teaching Carolyn how to line dance.

I break out into laughter. Not at them, but with some weird mixture of amusement and relief and ... I don't know.

What this is, in front of me, is one of the most beautiful things I've ever seen in my life. It's my mom, beaming from ear to ear as if an entire semi-truck has been lifted from her shoulders and she's throwing her head back, screaming in relief. Until this moment, I don't think I truly realized just how hard those years of job searching was for her.

And my sister, the black eye all faded away, can sense it too. She's spinning and laughing, her hair whipping wildly around her shoulders. I want to fall to my knees with relief, but that seems too dramatic, and besides, it's all I can do to stand there in the entryway, a silent observer as the two of them twist and twirl around the tiny space, never bumping into the cabinets, the fridge, anything, their steps fluid, their bodies graceful.

This is what I've wanted, forever and ever. It was never about money or nice things. It was this. This moment of knowing we'd be okay. Of seeing my mom free, relaxed, her head tipped back to the skies even though she's inside a house with a cramped, low ceiling. *Alive.* Of knowing, once and for all, that Carolyn will make it out of here, will be stronger than ever.

The song finally ends and the spinning slows, and when my mom tips her head back, she's beaming at me. "Hey. Didn't hear you come in."

"Wonder why," I say, dropping my bag onto the couch. "Something smells good."

"Me and Carolyn made a pizza," she says. "It's Hawaiian if you want some."

"Sure, maybe in a little bit."

"Okay."

"How was your first day?"

When she grins, I think I could count all her teeth. "Amazing. I'm going to be in charge of twelve other maids, and the last supervisor left lots of notes and instructions before she quit to take care of her sick dad. I have my own office!"

"That's great," I say.

"It is. And the thing is, this place is different. Everyone in upper management at this hotel . . . they earned it. They really like to promote people. There's a future there. I could become more than a supervisor. I could become the hotel manager someday."

My eyes sting before I can blink. "Oh Mom," I say. Walking to her, I let her envelop me in a hug. "You deserve this."

Neither of us speak for a minute, and when I realize Carolyn is standing awkwardly to one side, I grab her and yank her in, and the three of us hug under the ugly bug-catcher light, basking in the glow of the future.

———————

"So where are we going exactly?" I ask, slamming the door of Olivia's car and following her down the sidewalk.

"You'll see," she says, slapping the crosswalk button.

It must have been waiting for us, because it flashes the *walk* symbol almost instantly.

"Can you believe we got a perfect hundred on our assignment?" she asks as we cross the street.

"We worked hard on it."

"I know, but I never get As. I'm stoked."

We approach the archways of Tacoma's Union Station. It's not even a train station anymore, just an elaborate brick building with iconic archways. Every time I see it I think of some bygone era, when riding trains was glamorous. I picture ladies with big traveling gowns and fancy trunks arriving by carriage, excited for some grand adventure.

I push away the image as Olivia leads me under the arches, the cool night air blowing my hair out of my face. Ahead, a bridge glows, awash with a rainbow of color.

The bridge of glass. Below it is the freeway, a neverending stream of cars. But here, the blown glass vases and flowers and butterflies and twists and turns of glass ... each piece of art is incased in its own clear cube. The walls of the bridge must be ten feet high, and the span of the bridge ...

I've been up here during the day before. I thought it was

pretty seeing the elaborate glassworks, which are almost like spun sugar. And I've passed by before in a car, drove right underneath and thought it looked nice all lit up.

But at night, up close and backlit, it's breathtaking.

"This is . . . " I say, my voice trailing off as I stop in front of one particularly large vase. It must be four feet tall by itself, but it's got a dozen blown-glass flowers, too, as if it's a whole flower arrangement.

"I know," Olivia says, her breath on my ear.

I turn, my back against the wall of glass displays. "Why are we here?" I ask. She can't have talked to Liam yet. I just saw him. So why all the secrecy?

She smiles. Pulling a single flower out of her pocket, she dramatically going down on one knee. She holds the flower out, and it looks identical to the one behind me—the blown glass flower in the vase.

"Zoey Thomasson, will you go to the Fall Fling with me?"

I stare, slack-jawed, unable to move.

She giggles. "Don't freak out. Everyone will think we're just friends. Girls dance together all the time at these things. In case you didn't notice, there's kind of a guy shortage at Annie Wright."

I swallow. "But it's in two weeks."

Olivia furrows her eyebrows. "I know."

I purse my lips. "Your brother just invited me to his home-coming dance. It's the same weekend."

It's like I stole the breath from her lungs. She goes from a goofy, on-one-knee pose to dropping down to sit on her heels, staring up at me from the ground. "Oh."

"I'm not going with him," I say.

"But you're his girlfriend. You have to go with him."

I laugh, and it comes out ugly and bitter. "No, Olivia, you were supposed to talk to him today! I don't want to be with him anymore. If you don't tell him, I will."

"But he's never going to forgive me! Don't you get that? He's never liked a girl before, not like he likes you. He deserves to be happy."

"But it's not *real*," I say. "Not like it is with us."

"He's going to hate me," she moans.

"Really, Olivia? You're chickening out? Are we just supposed to stay like this forever? Am I supposed to just be with both of you? When are you going to call it off? When I'm marching down the aisle with him?"

She finally climbs up off the cement floor so that we're eye to eye. "That's not fair."

"What is fair? Dating him forever so you don't have to take me away from him? So you can stay the perfect sister in the hopes you'll always remain best friends? News flash, Olivia—he's sick of your neediness. He told me he wants you to get your shit together."

I've gone too far. I know it instantly by the expression on her face. It's like she shuts down, recoils all at once, reels every last feeling, every confession, inside her iron walls. And when she looks into my eyes again, she's the old Olivia, the one who ruled our school with an iron fist, whose perfection gleams from every photo.

"You know what?" she says, her voice cracking. "Take the light rail or walk home or something. I'm so done with this."

I rush after her. "Stop!" I say, yanking her arm back.

She stops but doesn't turn around, not right away. She stares at the ground in front of us, struggling to pull herself together.

"This isn't what I wanted, you know," she says a moment later. "This isn't who I thought I was."

"And it's who I planned to be?"

"I don't know, but you're sure handling it better than me."

"You can still be perfect, and be…" My voice trails off. "This, too," I say, motioning between us. "Because *I* think you're perfect."

The ragged, strangled breath she takes catches me off guard. Flawless, composed Olivia is barely holding it together.

"I've lost so much over the last couple years. The house I grew up in. My parents. Ava. And now you want me to go home and tell my brother I'm taking you away. Liam never cares about girls, and he cares about you. And if I take that from him, he's going to hate me. I'm going to lose him like I've lost everything else."

"I never had any of those things to begin with," I say, smiling sadly through my tears.

"Sorry," she whispers.

I reach out to touch Olivia's arm, but then she's backing away, her eyes still trained on me. She stares for a long, lingering moment, as if to memorize what I look like, out here beside the blown glass artwork.

And then she spins on her heel and runs off, leaving me standing on that bridge, the freeway traffic rushing by below.

OLIVIA

The next day, I'm sitting on the little window seat in my room, staring out at the water and wondering how it is I screwed things up so badly.

I ran away from Zoey the second she pushed. She wanted to end things with Liam, and I knew it was the right thing to do, but I freaked.

I exhale, and my breath fogs the glass. Then I pick up my phone and call her. Again.

It rings twice, then goes to voicemail, so I know she's screening my calls. If her phone was off, it wouldn't have rung at all.

She wasn't even at school today. I only went to school to see her, and she wasn't there.

"Hi, you've reached Zoey. Leave a message."

The beep comes, and for a long second I don't speak. The lump in my throat makes it seem impossible. I swallow it down. "Hey, Zoey," I say. "Look, I don't know what I'm doing any more, okay?"

My lip trembles and I realize how much I can't afford to lose her. How much I need her.

How much I care about her. I couldn't sleep last night, I just kept replaying the same thing over and over—that moment she said, *I choose you*, followed by the way her face crumpled when I left her there.

"I've never felt like this about anyone. It's terrifying. But I can't lose you. Give me another chance, please. Just don't give up on me yet. I'll talk to him, okay? Just tell me you'll still be there once I do."

I end the call and drop my phone into my lap, still staring out at the driveway. I wipe away the one tear that trails down my cheek.

A knock comes then and I jump, bumping my forehead against the glass before I turn to see my brother standing in the open doorway.

As our eyes lock, I know.

He knows.

He overheard the call.

His eyes search mine, boring into me. He steps into my room, then walks closer and sits at the edge of the bed, all without looking away. It's like he expects the answers to be written in my eyes.

"Just say it," I say.

He rubs his hair with one hand, then drops his hand back to his side. "Are you and Zoey more than friends?"

"We were," I say, sniffling. "And I know that makes me a really shitty sister because you liked her first."

"Have you dated other girls?" he asks.

I finally break our eye contact and look at the lines left in the carpet from the vacuum cleaner. I dig my toes into the deep pile. "No."

"Hey," he says. "Look at me."

I glance up again.

"I don't care, that you're ... you know."

I can't speak.

"But, I mean, it would have been cool if it wasn't a girl *I* was dating ... "

I can't help it. I laugh, and then it makes me want to cry.

"Are you in love with her?" Liam asks.

"Are you?" I counter.

He breathes deeply, leaning back on his hands on my bed. "I like her. I really do. But if she was pissed at *me*, I don't think I'd be moping in my room like ... " He swirls his finger around my room. "Like this."

I nod.

"Has *she* dated girls before?" he asks.

I shake my head.

"So you two just kind of ... '

"Fell into it."

"Huh," he says, as if struggling to wrap his head around it.

"I know, it's weird."

He shrugs. "Nah. Just ... unexpected."

I nod. "Yes. Definitely unexpected."

"Has it been going on the whole time I was dating her?"

I shake my head. "Not really. Just since the lake."

He nods slowly, staring at where my toes disappear into the carpeting. "Why didn't you tell me?"

I lean back, feeling the cool pane of glass on my back. "Because I thought you'd be pissed. I've been sneaking around with her, and she was *your* girlfriend first. And then you come home and tell me how amazing she is, and how am I supposed to tell you?"

Liam leans back too, resting his palms against my bed. "You use words, Olivia. Like the ones you're spouting right now."

I stand up and walk past him to my dresser. My hands slide down the strand of pearls draped around the corner of my mirror. "I'm not like you, Liam."

"I don't know about that. Sounds like we're both into girls."

I laugh again, not because the joke is all that funny, but because the relief at the way he's taking all of this is almost more than I can handle.

"I thought you'd be mad."

"Bewildered. Surprised. I'm ... " He trails off, and I glance over my shoulder. He puts one hand next to his temple and makes an explosion motion, like "mind blown" is the word he's looking for.

I turn around and lean against the dresser. "What happened to us, Liam? We used to be so ... "

And then, just as I say "close," he says "similar."

I furrow my brow. "We were never that similar."

"Sure we were. We played on the same T-ball team as kids, and we both sucked at it. We both were obsessed with *Pound Puppies* and we used to pretend all of our stuffed dogs came from the pound. We both wanted to be in the church play but neither of us had the guts to try out. Every Christmas, every birthday, we'd get the same gifts. A red bike for you, a blue one for me. A red sled for you, a blue one for me. A red stuffed bear for you, a blue one for me."

He seems to be staring at some swirl in carpet, smiling softly to himself. "The thing is, we grew up, Liv. I found the person I wanted to become, and I can't be someone else just to stay close to you. "

"I've never asked you to be someone else."

"No? You didn't force me to go to those art museums in Paris last summer?"

"It's because Mom wouldn't let us run around a foreign town alone."

"You don't try to make me go see subtitled movies every Friday, even though I'd rather see a Bruce Willis movie?"

"It's tradition."

"You don't make fun of my skateboarding?"

My jaw drops. "I'm just joking around."

"You want me to be who I used to be, Liv."

"I don't want you to be someone else! I just want you to be my best friend!"

Liam sighs. "You're never going to lose me. You just have to let our relationship evolve. *You* have to evolve. And if that means being... whatever you are with Zoey, then be that person.

But stop holding yourself back. You're never going to be twelve years old again, when everything was perfect."

My throat feels raw, and just breathing hurts.

"Look," he says, standing up. "I love you. But I promised Rusty I'd meet him at Foss. So I'm going to get going and leave you to … mope or eat ice cream or whatever girls do."

I smile, hoping my eyes aren't glittering with tears. I'm too overwhelmed right now to handle him staying and telling me more hard truths.

"Thanks, Liam."

And then he leaves me.

ZOEY

I haven't moved in hours.

I feel like I'm weighed down, that my limbs are filled with sand, and it takes too much effort to get out of bed. I skipped school, even, and I haven't done that in years. The idea of seeing Olivia and knowing that she won't just freaking talk to her brother so we can be together is more than I want to handle.

On my dresser, my cell chirps again. Another message. But I don't need to talk to her, not if it's just going to end with the same result: Olivia too scared to be together, too scared to hurt Liam.

"Someone in a very tall Jeep just pulled into the driveway," Carolyn says from the doorway of our room.

I sit up and glance out the window.

"It's Liam," I say, my stomach twisting. What's he doing here? We don't have any plans. And the mere *idea* of having to fake it again, pretend to be his girlfriend, is more than I can deal with right now.

Carolyn follows me out into the living room, weaving her way between the junk all over the floor. Mom suggested we donate as much old stuff as possible so we don't have to pack it up when we move to a new apartment, and Carolyn has taken to the project with gusto.

I think she's more excited than I am about getting out of Hilltop. Mom said the new apartment isn't anything fancy, but it's clean and bright and safe. And best of all, it's in a different school district for Carolyn. Since Annie Wright is a private school, I won't have to transfer.

I put up a hand to stop my sister. "Hey, where do you think you're going?"

"To say hi to Liam!"

"Um, no. I need to talk to him alone."

She pouts but goes to the couch and plops down. I wait until she puts her feet up on the coffee table before I go out the front door.

Liam's just about to step up onto the front porch.

"Uh, hey, what's up?" I ask, shutting the front door behind me.

He holds something out to me, and when I put my hand out, palm-up, he drops a yellow Post-it note onto it.

"What's this?"

"The access code to our building."

I raise a brow.

"I'm going to be gone for the next two hours. I suggest you go talk to Olivia."

I just kind of stand there, like some freaking statue, my mind moving about as slow as molasses.

"I know what you guys are," he says.

"Oh," I say dumbly. My heartbeat reaches a crescendo, the beat so loud I'm sure he can hear it.

"You could have told me," he says when I stay silent.

I nod, because of course he's right and of course he's entirely, completely wrong.

"So, she actually told you? Everything?" I finally say.

"No. I overheard her leaving you a message."

My stomach sinks as the disappointment sets in. I'd actually thought maybe she'd done the right thing and told him herself. "Oh."

"Why are you mad at her?"

"Because she's more worried about being the perfect sister than she is about being with me. She couldn't just talk to you. And I was tired of pretending. You're amazing, but you're not ... you're not Olivia."

It's surreal to be standing in front of Liam and admitting this aloud.

"It's who Olivia is," he says. "You can't expect her to change overnight."

"I know," I say. "Maybe I'm expecting too much."

He nods.

"Why are you taking this so well?" I ask. But I'm not entirely surprised. Liam has always been pretty unflappable. It's weird, really, that he's related to Olivia.

"I don't know. I like you. And I love my sister. If you two being together is what makes you happiest, and is what makes her happiest, then so be it. I'll just have to hope there are *two* girls in the world as cool as you are."

"Oh."

"Anyway, like I said, I have things to do. Use the code. Go see her."

And then, before I can say anything else, he spins on his heel and strides across the patchy brown lawn to his Jeep.

"Hey, Liam?" I call after him.

He pauses, turning back to me.

"Thank you. For … everything. You're a good guy."

He nods, giving me a smile before he climbs into his Jeep, and drives away.

I stand on the front porch and watch until he disappears around the corner. Then I duck my head back into the living room, only to find the couch empty. Carolyn is standing at the window peeking through an opening in the drapes.

"I'm going to be gone for like a half hour, okay?" I say.

"Okay, fine."

"Don't bug Mom, all right? I think she's reading in the bathtub. She deserves a break. If you leave her alone, I'll bring you back some of those stupid pickle-flavored chips you like." I grab my purse off the side table near the door.

She brightens. "Deal."

"Work on your homework or something," I call out as I shut the door.

OLIVIA

"I don't care if you're still pissed at me. I'm not going to let you skip the dance," Ava says, propping her hand on her hip. "It's not allowed. So let's just forget about our little argument and go to the mall and pick out some dresses."

"It's not a little argument," I say. "I'm only talking to you because you needed your Dolce jacket back. Now you have it. You can go home."

"I don't understand why you're not talking to me anymore."

"Because I have nothing left to say to you, Ava!"

She pouts. "We've been best friends since the third grade. You can't just break up with me. Friends don't break up."

"You don't even see that you're wrong. So, yeah, I can break up with you."

"Why do you even care about Zoey? She's not worth your

time. If you want to adopt something, go to the shelter and pick out a dog."

The words sting, crawling under my skin and sticking there. I'd once thought something similar about Zoey, that night she came home with Liam. Jesus, had I always been as judgmental as Ava?

"Fuck you, Ava," I say, jutting a thumb over my shoulder at the door. "And get out of my house."

Her jaw drops. "What the hell is even wrong with you? Do you really like her that much?"

She's moving closer, step after step after step, as if she thinks I'll edge away.

Instead, I draw myself up. "*Yes*," I grind out. "I really do. And until you come to terms with that, and until you apologize to her and *mean it*, we have nothing to say."

Ava goes rigid, glaring into my eyes. The condo falls silent.

And then there's slow clapping, somewhere behind me.

I whirl around. It's Zoey, the slightest of smiles playing on her lips, her eyes sparkling.

I can see it, the rage and frustration boiling beneath Ava's skin, and I wonder, really, how I ever saw her as my best friend. It was there all along, our differences. She's never cared about the future, about who we would become. She never wanted to work together on homework and projects when I asked—not when she could find a guy to hang out with or a store to shop in.

Whatever we had, it was entirely surface level.

"Goodbye, Ava," I say, and while the words start strong, they end up as a whisper.

She shakes her head as if she pities me, and then spins on her heel and strides out the door.

She slams it so hard it rattles the pictures on the wall, but then it's silence.

I gaze at Zoey. "How much did you hear?" I ask. My bravado fails me as I glance downward.

"Enough."

"Enough to what?"

"Believe in you. Maybe I pushed too hard with Liam, but what you just did . . . was brave. Thank you."

"Really?" I look up at her.

"I talked to Liam too," she says. "I know you didn't mean to tell him, but at least he knows about us now. And I guess that's good enough."

"You really talked to him?"

"Yeah. And I'm not with him anymore."

I twist a strand of hair around my finger. "So . . . if I tell you I made a mistake, that I don't want to lose you . . . "

"I would ask if it's too late to buy tickets to the Fall Fling," Zoey says.

I look up, relief barreling through me. "You're too forgiving," I say. "Lucky for me."

"It's not like I have it all figured out, either," she says, reaching over and untangling my finger from my hair, then clasping my hand in hers. "I just want to know you're in. For the long haul. Because this isn't going to be easy."

I purse my lips, nodding with absolute sincerity. "Yes. I'm in."

Zoey grins from ear to ear. "Good. Because if we're going to go to this dance, I'm going to need a dress. And I'm really bad at picking out dresses."

ZOEY

— *Ten Months Later* —

I raise a hand, shielding my eyes from the late afternoon sun, squinting against the glare. My shoulders are hot, and I know I should slather on another layer of sunscreen, but I can't tear my eyes from the boat ripping toward me. It's pulling someone, a small set of roostertails spraying into the air.

It can't be. There's no way she picked it up that fast.

I squint, trying to get a clear view of the gangly figure on the skies. Finally, the boat turns slightly and the skier swings out from behind it, the tow-rope going taut, the skier sliding out from behind the wake and popping up over the little wave.

My jaw drops.

Carolyn.

Even from a distance, even with the glare and the waves, she's unmistakable.

"Holy shit," I mutter under my breath, watching as she bends her knees, making it over the wake without falling.

The boat slows and she somehow knows what this means, dropping the triangle-shaped tow handle.

She skids across the surface for one, two, three seconds until the momentum slows, then drops into the water, yards shy of the dock.

The tips of her skis poke out of the surface, just like her life jacket, and she grins so wide I can't believe her face doesn't crack. "THAT. WAS. AWESOME."

She busts out into laughter, and I can't help but grin in response.

"Having fun?" I drop down to sit on the dock.

"Yeah." She kind of doggie paddles, trying to get closer to me without taking the skis off. "BEST DAY EVER!" she screams, tipping her head back.

I laugh, pointing my toes so I can kick at the water, spraying it toward her.

The dopey grin drops from her face "But really, thanks for bringing me."

"Hey, you finished your first semester at Lowell with all pluses! I figured I could bring you out here as a reward."

"I can't even believe Mom said yes."

I grin. "I'm eighteen now, so I'm a legitimate adult chaperone. Plus, I'm pretty sure she wanted to spend the weekend with Charlie."

"Ugh," Carolyn says, sticking her tongue out.

I laugh. "Oh, come on. He's a cool guy. Give him a chance."

"Maybe."

I splash water at her with my toe again. "Hey! I mean it."

"Fine, he's kind of cool. He took me and Mom to the Lakewood Theater last weekend. You know they have seats that recline? Made of leather. You just push a button and a footrest slides out."

I smile. "Sounds awesome."

"They are. You should buy recliners for your apartment with Olivia. Then maybe I'll visit."

"Hey now," a voice says behind me. Olivia's footsteps are quiet on the planks. "We picked a loft that's close to you guys. The least you could do is visit, recliners or not."

"Yeah, and I picked UW Tacoma because of you," I add. "You're pretty much required to drag Mom over once a week for dinner."

Carolyn frowns. I know she's still getting used to the idea of me moving out, but I can't quite bring myself to feel bad when I know I'm staying so close. "I still don't see why you have to move at all," she mutters.

"For the 'college experience,'" Liv says, grinning. "And because my parents are bankrolling it."

I laugh. It's true, though. We're doing our lower level classes at the Tacoma campus, and then maybe if we're feeling adventurous we'll go to the Seattle campus for our upper level stuff, really get the experience of going to a big college. But since Olivia's parents had already agreed to bankroll campus housing, they kinda paid for our place at Harmon Lofts, these really cool apartments in a converted furniture factory on the same block as the college.

As much as I wanted to reject their offer, resist it on principle... I'm getting used to saying, "Yes please," and "Thank you" instead.

Besides, I'll have to help Olivia with homework practically every night, so I think we're almost even.

"Hand me your skis," I say to Carolyn as she gets closer.

She pops them off, holding them up at such an angle that I can grab the curved tips.

Free of the skies, she turns on her back and floats leisurely toward the ladder around the side of the dock just as the speed boat completes its loop and heads back toward us. I let my eyes drift to Liam, and to the girl sitting beside him.

"So do we like this new Jennifer girl or do we not like her?" I ask, sliding the skis onto the dock.

"I haven't decided yet," Olivia says. "She's studying Poli Sci. Seems... smart."

"She sucks at skiing," I say, giggling.

"Liam claims she's more of a wakebarder," Olivia says. "I think skateboarding translates better to that than skiing."

I chew on my lip to keep from laughing. "I kind of liked when she did the splits, though. I kept waiting for her to just *let go* of the tow rope."

Olivia leans against me as she laughs, so hard she almost pushes me off the side of the dock. "I was hoping Liam would tow her in a complete loop before she gave up. Who knew she was so flexible?"

The boat slows, approaching the shore.

"She seems cool, though. So far."

"Yeah. We'll see."

Olivia twists around as Carolyn climbs up the ladder. "Hey, you wanna make banana boats tonight?"

Carolyn, still dripping wet, strides across the dock, leaving wet footprints behind. "What's a banana boat?"

I can't help but grin as Olivia meets my eyes. "You've never had a banana boat?" she asks.

"Now that is a travesty," I say.

"Come on. Let's go up and get the ingredients ready." Olivia stands up and holds her hand out to pull me to my feet.

"You coming, Carolyn?" I ask, turning back to her.

"Nah. I'm going lie here and dry off."

"Okay."

Olivia and I walk up to the cabin and climb the creaky steps. At the top, I stop at the railing and stare out at the beauty of the lake.

"I love this place," I say.

Olivia comes up beside me, putting her arm around my shoulders and squeezing me up against her. "I do too. Especially now that you're here with *me*."

And when she kisses my temple, I close my eyes, listening to the lake and her breath and wondering how it is that everything ended up exactly how it should.

© Amber Sheree Photography

About the Author

Amanda Grace is a pseudonym for Mandy Hubbard. She's the author of *But I Love Him*, *In Too Deep*, and *The Truth About You & Me*, written as Amanda Grace, and several novels under her own name. She lives near Seattle, Washington, where she watches a lot of sports (Go Sounders!) and wastes too much time on Twitter. Learn more at MandyHubbard.com.